MEGALODON GULF

SAM M. PHILLIPS

SEVEREDPRESS

MEGALODON GULF

Copyright © 2025 by Sam M. Phillips

WWW.SEVEREDPRESS.COM

ISBN: *978-1-923165-52-6*

1

Arafura Sea, off the north coast of Australia, 1952

The boat was tossed about like a cork in the turbulent sea. Crests of huge waves slashed the deck, flashing white like exposed blades in the pale moonlight. Inside the boat's creaking timbers, the crew huddled around the cabin's mess table, nestled in like fragile eggs. The strain on the faces of the men was plain—there was genuine concern the boat wouldn't hold it together through the storm.

"We make for the coast now, we've still got a decent catch," said one man, the texture of his bulbous nose matching the corn cob pipe he puffed at nervously.

"More importantly, we'll have our lives," said another, his eyes darting about nervously, his sharp rat-like teeth nibbling what little fingernails he had left after the long months of living on edge.

"But what type of lives will they be if we don't have money in our pockets? I'm not going back to the wife with a pittance," said the final man, whose vast bulk equalled that of the first two put together and more. A white cap with a black peak—worn by sea captains the world over—sat on his fat head, deflated and flat as a pancake.

"You just don't want to go back to the wife, period," said Corn Cob.

"I don't want to go back to my wife because she's always on her period," said Fat Head, his massive bulk rolling like an avalanche as he let out a sigh.

"Or has a headache," sniggered Rat Teeth.

Fat Head rolled his eyes up at the mouldy ceiling of the cabin as if asking for deliverance from a stain there which looked a little like Jesus.

"And money will fix that?" asked Corn Cob, puffing thoughtfully, filling the small room with smoke.

"It'll keep me in grog and get my end wet down the cathouse," said Fat Head, waving a meaty paw around to clear the air.

"That's what I mean. We've already got enough fish on ice in the hull for that."

"But not for that and to keep the wife off my back while I keep some other man's on hers."

Rat Teeth tittered at this, thrusting his hips against the underside of the table.

Corn Cob said, "If that's your worry, it's been long enough out at sea as it is."

Fat Head shook his fat head. "And not enough fish biting."

"You'll not get more bites back at port, I'll promise you that."

"Money is the finest bait."

"And more's the pity we didn't have enough of that to load us out with the proper stuff we need for the actual catch we're chasing."

"Women?" said Rat Teeth.

Corn Cob bopped him on the head with his pipe. "No, you idiot. Spanish mackerel."

"But this is Australia, not Spain."

"Didn't quite twist the light bulb all the way in when they installed you, did they?"

"I know we're out here for mackerel, if that's what you mean. Good Aussie mackerel."

"I think the Indonesians, or even the Papuans would have just as much claim to them as us."

"Not on your life. We're in Australian waters still," said Fat Head, slapping a chart thumbtacked to the wall, drooping at the torn corners. The island continent of their birth looked like a faded grey shadow amidst pastel blue oceans, already lost to them.

"Then let's head back to Australian *land* while we've still got a boat to carry us there," said Corn Cob.

"Fish, fish, fish!" said Rat Teeth, again humping the table.

"I think you're outvoted there, cobber," said Fat Head. "There's barely enough mackerel in the hold to cover our expenses, let alone fund another trip out. We go back now and we're as stuck there as we're stuck here."

"So, we wait for the fish to bite with no good bait?" asked Corn Cob.

"We could..." started Fat Head, easing himself out of his seat like an engorged seal flopping off an iceberg. Once clear of the table, he moved more freely, as did his thoughts. They rocked back and forth in his head like bilge water in the reeking hull, which sloshed beneath the floor he stood on. The man's sea legs meant he was always level despite his unwieldy size, but this didn't mean his thinking wasn't swaying back and forth between possibilities, weighing the odds. He snapped his fingers with a conman's smile. "We could double down, go for the big ones."

"And what exactly does that mean?" said Corn Cob, tapping the ash from his pipe and reaching for the tobacco pouch to pack another. It would be yet another in a long string he'd smoked that night, fretting for their safety and knowing the captain wouldn't let him off the line that easily. He was hooked, like they all were, drawn on by the hopes of a bigger score.

"We bait up the lines with the Spanish mackerel," said Fat Head, grabbing the pipe out of Corn Cob's hand and waving it about with a flourish, like a general drawing his sword emphatically as he revealed a cunning stratagem.

Corn Cob reached desperately for the pipe, his only life raft on this ship of madmen. Rat Teeth tapped his foot nervously, sucking on a longneck beer—his own personal solace as he put up no resistance to the plan.

Fat Head made a peace offering, extending the pipe to Corn Cob, who snatched it back and said, "Those mackerel are money in the bag. They're our only catch. You'd risk that, and for what? What exactly are these big ones?"

"Big ol' sharks, of course," said Fat Head.

Rat Teeth sucked at his rat teeth. Corn Cob loaded his pipe with tobacco, trying to focus on the taste and the imminent rush of nicotine more than the words spoken.

"All opposed?" asked Fat Head, glowering at the two other men. He knew his audience, knew better than to ask for those in favour. This way the others could be passive, subdued and comforted by their addictions, which held them like lovers and soothed them. Smoked filled the cabin as Corn Cob puffed away, and Rat Teeth stopped sucking his teeth, reached for another beer, sucking on it instead like a baby at its bottle.

"It's decided then," said Fat Head, slapping his hands together in triumph. "Let's turn in and get some rest. We've a big day ahead of us tomorrow."

Outside, the storm grew worse and lashed the boat with rain. Wind threw it about as waves lifted the hull and dumped it down again. Well aware the boat might give way any moment, awakening them to a violent, drowning death—or, alternatively, a slower one if they didn't catch something—the men went to their bunks, to sleep if they could, but with minds blazing at the possibilities, as well as the risks.

***

The men were up before the dawn, hauling the mackerel from cold storage below onto deck to be butchered. By the time the sun rose on the eastern horizon—blazing at them like an accusing searchlight catching them in the act—they were covered in gore like axe murderers, their cleavers hanging slack in hands sore from hacking up fish. The bloody chunks of fish lay in a huge pile which dominated the deck with its bulk, as well as its stench, but the work was far from done.

"Get the lines out," said Fat Head, slapping Rat Teeth on the butt with his crusted cleaver. The man scampered away to work the derrick overhead, where the lines were bundled up in a net.

"Hooks, hooks!" Fat Head cried, as if calling for the heads of his enemies, brandishing the cleaver menacingly. Corn Cob was slower to comply, weary from the work and lack of sleep, having been up late worrying. Fat Head hadn't got much sleep either, but he'd had plenty to drink so was numb to fatigue, his mind ablaze with the blood which sloshed across the deck, mixing with sea water into a foul, salty brew which frothed around their gumboots. He kicked at it as if it were a mongrel dog, sending it on its way, only for it to return, the same dog wanting to be fed, on his corpse if it had to.

"You'll not take me yet," Fat Head growled at it, then to the sea beyond, "You hear me?"

"He's bloody mad," muttered Corn Cob as he fished out the hooks, laying them in heavy rows of clinking metal on top of a box.

"Yeah, but those sharks are going to fetch us a pretty penny," said Rat Teeth, tittering with delight. He'd not slept much either, but his mind was not filled with dread as much as with visions of the money to be had, and all the beer and prostitutes it would buy. It would keep him awash for six months or more, and he wouldn't have to go out on a boat again for a while. All he had to do was ignore the fact he was drenched in blood and fish guts right now, and one day he wouldn't have to be drenched in blood and fish guts any longer.

"Just pussy and piss," he said, as if Corn Cob had been following along with his thoughts. Instead, it was said in isolation and made him sound deranged. He looked around, nervously sucking his teeth.

"You're bloody mad and all," said Corn Cob with a shake of his head. He began the arduous task of affixing the heavy hooks to the stout lines, his fingers numb in their rubber gloves from the hours of hacking up frozen corpses. He was wondering how it had come to this. His life was never meant to be this dirty and disgusting, but unlike Rat Teeth, he saw no way out—there was no big score at the end which would free him from the drudgery forever.

Earn more money, you just spend it, and you're back where you started.

He considered giving it all up and going back to the Tweed Shire to at least be near his aging parents and his brothers. But all that would accomplish would be to trade the cleaver and hook for the machete, joining his brothers in the fields harvesting sugar cane. Not for the first time he cursed his own brown skin and the skin of the white man. He couldn't direct his anger at Rat Teeth—the fellow was too stupid and used up to be his oppressor—but he could turn it on Fat Head.

"You don't even own this ship," he said under his breath, aimed at the captain but not for his ears. "You're just as much a slave to it as I am. The company takes its share, and what's left for us?"

He picked up a hunk of mackerel. Threading it onto a hook he looked at the rest of the pile of meat. "They have all the profits to reinvest while we take home one small portion."

"Yeah, profits, think of the profits," said Rat Teeth sincerely, taking to his work with a will. He was like a machine when he got to thinking about the money that could be made, and this made him a born fisherman. No time to waste on a ship when there's fish to be caught, because who wants to waste more time than they have to on a stinking little tub like this?

Corn Cob looked around at the sea. It stretched forever, not another boat in sight. His eyes turned to the surface of the water and his thoughts to the harvest which could be gained from the multitude of life hiding behind that opaque barrier.

"Come on, come on, back to work," said Fat Head, jabbing at the pile of defrosting fish with his cleaver.

Corn Cob looped one of the big hooks through his fingers so it protruded between his knuckles. Fat Head saw him mentally manipulating it through his fat head, and some of the blood drained from his drink-reddened features.

"Alright, all hands to it with a will," said Fat Head, a little less enthusiastically, the threat having penetrated the thick fog of his grog-addled mind. He chopped the cleaver into the wooden top of a box and grabbed a hunk of meat. "You'll see. The sharks will go crazy for it." He pushed the half-frozen morsel onto a waiting hook and pulled the line along to receive the next.

"We've already gone mad for it, and we've barely had a nibble," said Corn Cob.

"Think of the money," said Rat Teeth out of the side of his mouth.

"What do you think I was talking about?"

***

"Chum the waters!" screamed Fat Head, as if he were calling for a human sacrifice. It wasn't such a stretch to think of it as such. There was a pile of fish guts on the deck, stinking in the hot sun, ready to be offered up to the shark gods. Corn Cob and Rat Teeth, their rubber overalls already befouled beyond human endurance, leant their shoulders to the mass and pushed it towards the open gate at the back of the boat.

Slowly, painfully, the rotting, bloody clot was cleared, a tumour being pulled from a body. It plopped into the water behind the boat with a disgusting organic sound, first in clumps, and then in a heaving, boiling lump which rolled about as it fought to stay afloat like a stricken swimmer. Unable to save itself, the sacrificed flesh came apart as it was churned up by the boat's wake. Blood seeped from it as if from a grievous wound and spread in an inky red trail behind the boat.

"Yes," growled Fat Head. He spread his arms wide as if he himself were the sacrifice, a Jesus on his cross, the silhouette of the big man mirrored in the stretched beams of the outriggers extending either side of the boat. These metal spars held the vast lines of baited hooks and strained under their weight—and this was before they even caught anything. Corn Cob shuddered to think what they'd be like if they actually succeeded in this mad endeavour and got loaded up with sharks.

The three of them stood watching the water behind the boat for a long time, the dark crimson stain of the chum floating far behind now, an island of horror sinking beneath the waves.

"Fuck this, let's get a drink," said Fat Head. Rat Teeth smiled and clapped his gore-smeared gloves together. Corn Cob frowned, staring at the horizon as if it were a curtain falling on the final chapter of his life.

***

The cabin reeked to high heaven, even more than usual, but the three of them didn't care anymore. They'd stripped off their blood-encrusted overalls and gumboots, but it wasn't like the butcher's work they'd been doing hadn't seeped down to the clothes beneath. It had even entered the pores of their skin. It became a permanent perfume which was impossible to banish with soap and scrubbing. Little wonder fishermen had to pay for sex, for what woman would want them now they had been pickled by the briny sea and baptised in the blood of its deep-dwelling denizens?

Not that it mattered, for the beers had been downed by the dozen and further rounds rejected in favour of the harder stuff. Rum flowed like urine from a god's cock into their mouths, or so Fat Head liked to joke in his more bombastic, grog-sodden moments.

For a while, the three of them forgot their worries, forgot they had thrown away the only viable catch they had on a pipedream. They forgot the lines behind the boat, trailing long in the water as the engine chugged on, the steering wheel held on its course with a length of tied rope. It would take them days before they hit anything resembling land on their present course, and any other boats that might be in their way, well, fuck those idiots and all, Rat Teeth said, and they'd all laughed.

No concern for the wellbeing of the boat he was responsible for had penetrated Fat Head's thick skull for many hours, and Corn Cob had sucked down so many pipes he was an asphyxiated victim of a house fire, near unconscious on the floor. Rat Teeth tittered and danced to music only he heard, Fat Head tapping his feet on the floor without rhythm as he slowly slid down his chair to join Corn Cob beneath the table. Rat Teeth stumbled on their corpse-like bodies and fell beside them, banging his head on the table's edge as he went. His eyes flittered and closed as he tried feebly to rise. He quickly gave up, a dullard's smile of tiny, sharp teeth showing through his thin lips. A trail of smoke rose from Corn Cob's corn cob pipe, but the man no longer sucked it down and it rose like a warning signal into the air, but with no one to take heed of it.

The boat rocked back and forth, lulling them to sleep like a mother cradling a baby. They were tugged down into the depths of full, blackout unconsciousness just as in the depths of the sea something stirred, sniffing the scent of blood in the water.

***

The crew awoke with a jolt as the boat was tugged on hard, a giant yanking their chains to pull them up short from their blissful oblivion. Corn Cob smacked his head as he rose, Rat Teeth bit down hard on the corn cob pipe which had somehow rolled into his open, snoring mouth, and Fat Head let out a groan which sounded suspiciously like a death rattle as he bit his tongue with his blunt, rotten teeth.

They didn't get to their feet so much as they were hurled upright as the ship listed heavily to one side, rolling them over and planting them flat against one wall. A huge avalanche of bottles followed them in a shrieking explosion of broken glass. Then the ship rocked the other way, as if a dog were worrying the hull in its teeth like a bone, shaking it back and forth. The three men stumbled backwards, and would have fallen if they hadn't been thrown up against the table.

"Fuck, cursed bloody fuck," said Fat Head, dancing around in his woollen socks, already wet with booze and urine, now joined by patches of red as he cut up his feet on the shards of glass.

Rat Teeth was nimbler, jumping up to grab a railing overhead and hang there like a gibbering monkey. Corn Cob grasped his head, hurt more in his hangover haze by the brilliant shattering cacophony of first the glasses breaking, and afterwards by the agonising sliding grind of the shards sloshing back and forth on the floor as the deck heaved beneath them. He fell up rather than climbed the stairs in an effort to escape, Fat Head coming after him, leaving bloody footprints in his wake. Rat Teeth dropped down onto the table—the one place now devoid of glass—and got down on his belly, his fingers shaking as familiar tremors started to wrack his body. He reached down, fumbling through the scree of broken bottles in an attempt to find one still intact enough to contain some alcohol.

He sighed with relief when he found one, and downed it despite the fact the contents were now mixed with salty water and tinged inky red with the captain's blood. When he'd finished sucking on the bottle, he pulled it away to realise its rim had been snapped off and the sharp edge of the glass had sliced his lip. Now his own blood ran down his face and joined the disgusting mix on the floor. He wiped at it in disgust, but didn't have time to think much of it as Fat Head bellowed down at him from up on deck.

"Get your arse up here, boy," said the captain.

Rat Teeth didn't much like being called boy, but at forty, he was the youngest of the three, and while his teeth might be ratty, he still had most of them, unlike the other two fishermen. Shrugging, he leapt nimbly to grab a railing by the stairs, and missed despite his confidence, because his body was still wracked by tremors. His hands grabbed empty air and he cursed himself and all the gods of the sea as he fell back into the waiting bed of glass, which opened its arms like a lover for this forlorn alcoholic man, embracing him with all its jagged pain which cut both ways, something he'd grown used to over the years but still hurt.

**

"What in the hell is that racket down there?" said Fat Head, shaking his many chins in consternation and glancing back at the hatch. It couldn't hold his attention long though, for there were far more interesting sights up on deck.

Corn Cob pulled tobacco out of his pocket, loading up his pipe thoughtfully as he too pondered sun and sea. He popped the wooden stem of the pipe between his teeth and pat down the chest of his sweat stained shirt, hoping to find matches there even though the garment lacked the necessary pockets.

"Looks like you could use a light," said Fat Head, swallowing hard so that his chins undulated. He produced a book of matches, handed them to Corn Cob, who took them and tilted his head to the side to study the front of the packet.

"The Imperial Hotel, Murwillumbah. Pouring pints in cane country since 1931," he read out loud. He sighed and opened the book of matches, pulled one out, and struck it. The flame flared dramatically and danced in the sea breeze. Corn Cob stuffed it into the pipe and sucked to get it going, leaving the match in there, not caring anymore. "Makes you long for home, doesn't it?"

He took a long draught of the smoke, inhaling deeply and savouring it as if it were the smoke off the cane fires in harvesting season.

"Oh, we'll be going home alright. Look at the strain on those lines," said Fat Head, gawping with his mouth open, the lips unmoving so that the words came from deep in his throat like a ventriloquist. It was like he was trying to swallow whole any and all fish that might

12

suddenly fly out of the sea and into his greedy, waiting mouth, and he wasn't going to miss any opportunity to do so.

"You think that's what this means, do you?" asked Corn Cob, tilting his head at an even greater angle to make his sight level with the horizon. The entire boat was listing heavily, pulled down by the lines so that the stern was riding very low in the water. The sun glistened off the sea in a sparkling array of diamonds, the seagulls squawked overhead amidst lazy clouds, and it all seemed so idyllic that it panged at Corn Cob that alarm bells were sounding in his head, ones apparently only he could hear.

"They're loaded up," said Fat Head, plucking at one of the taut lines as if it were the string of some heavenly harp, playing music that would lead him to paradise.

Corn Cob frowned. "Yes," he said. "Too heavily. If any more jump on the bait they'll drag us under. Not to mention we don't even know what's on the other end. Could be a bloody whale for all we know."

"Whale? You daft bugger. They don't eat mackerel. I'm telling you, we're rich. They're sharks, can't you see?"

"I can't see shit yet," said Corn Cob, approaching the tail end of the boat with caution. He looked over. The water was dark and opaque, but he could see some type of ominous silhouette moving down there, perhaps more than one. "There's *something* on the lines."

"Of course there is," said Fat Head, wincing as he plodded forward. His cut up feet bothered him. He fetched around for some boots, and finding none, cursed and stomped his feet petulantly, which made him howl with frustration and pain.

"Bit of salty water will do those wounds good," said Rat Teeth, crawling up on deck, covered in cuts himself.

"Is that so, smart arse?" said Fat Head. "Why don't you go ahead and roll around in it if you're so keen on your health?"

Before Corn Cob could tell him to definitely not do that, Rat Teeth sloshed around in the assorted briny, bloody filth sloshing about the deck, as if he were a happy pig in muck.

"You seem chipper," deadpanned Corn Cob.

"Hair of the dog that bit you," said Rat Teeth, flashing what looked more like a grimace than a smile.

"I could use a pull myself," said Fat Head, heading back for the cabin.

"I don't think that's such a good idea," said Corn Cob, pulling his pipe from his mouth and using it to indicate the general situation by waving it vaguely around in the air.

"Oh, right, the catch. But when didn't we go to work without a bit of a snifter under our belts?" said Fat Head, tugging his pants up around his enormous girth.

"Work? You think we're going to be able to draw in these lines?" said Corn Cob, incredulous. He grasped the nearest one. It was stiff like an iron rod, taut as a drawn bowstring.

"We'll get the derrick on them, winch them in."

The whole boat lurched as something heavy tugged on the lines. Corn Cob shook his head, and said, "I think whatever is on the line is winching us in."

***

Without the sense of urgency which Corn Cob felt the situation deserved, Rat Teeth and Fat Head went about first making themselves comfortable, changing into dry underclothes, patching wounds, and getting on their rubber overalls and boots—not to mention raiding the vast reserves of booze that was still intact below deck in an ice chest. No one bothered to clean up the broken glass though. Even Corn Cob was too distracted to do that. He turned down drink and smoked pipe after pipe, staring at the fishing lines getting tauter and tauter as they hauled at the boat, wondering who had caught who.

He patted the wooden chest he sat on like a soldier would stroke their weapon, trying to calm a desperate urge that had come over him, knowing his gut feeling was right but not yet ready to face it. In the chest was an axe. He just wasn't sure yet if he was going to have to use it.

***

The devastating blow came as Fat Head and Rat Teeth readied the derrick and started to drag in a line, but it wasn't the one any of them expected.

"Are you going to do any damned work?" Fat Head said to Corn Cob, who sat tapping his foot impatiently as he watched the line come in one agonising metre at a time, the winch straining and screaming with the herculean effort.

"I'm doing my job, don't you worry about that," said Corn Cob, squinting at the sun and wishing it would fuck off. He envied the other two the confidence they found in their bottles, and his hangover hadn't cleared to his liking, but he wouldn't leave his post, knowing he was the only one who could save them if he was right.

The hooks started to show above the water, and his guts churned nauseatingly as the blow landed like a knockout punch.

There was nothing on them.

"What in the hell?" said Fat Head, grabbing an empty hook as it came up. It had to be cut from the line to stop the winding line getting snagged in the derrick winch and it dropped to the deck with a clang like a muffled brass bell.

"Where's the shark?" said Rat Teeth, looking around as if the sea creature was just playing games, and having jumped off the hook, would sneak up on them from behind and give them a scare.

"Don't worry," said Corn Cob, tapping the ash from his pipe. "She's out there."

"She better be, with a whole bunch of her friends and all," said Fat Head, activating the winch to bring up another length of the still taut line. "There's got to be something snagged on it, look at the tension."

The line glistened with wetness in the sunlight, dancing about like a tightrope.

"That something better be a whole heap of sharks," said Rat Teeth.

Corn Cob laughed darkly at this, nodding along. He'd let himself give in totally to the fantasy playing out in his head. Call it a hunch, call it seaman's intuition—he knew something wasn't right.

"Let's hope it's just a whole heap of old boots," he said, continuing to chuckle without mirth, loading up the umpteenth pipe of the morning. He didn't light it yet, watching the line with anticipation as another hook emerged.

"Don't say that, you bloody mongrel," said Fat Head. But as the hook came out of the water there was, yet again, nothing on it.

"We have to have caught something," said Rat Teeth in exasperation as hook after hook came up without a catch. As they neared the end of the line, a big pile of hooks on the deck, they looked at each other with dawning horror, but each of them imagined a different scenario to fear.

For Fat Head it was the oblivion of a life of misery back on shore with his shrew of a wife nagging him to make more money. For Rat Teeth it was a sober reality, a fate worse than death, with no way of buying a bottle to numb the pain of existence.

But for Corn Cob it was one word, describing a spectre he'd conjured in his own mind he couldn't banish.

"Megalodon," he breathed.

***

"What the fuck did you just say?" said Fat Head, marching over to Corn Cob and knocking the pipe out of his mouth with a smack of his hand. It tumbled over the side of the boat and disappeared into the water. Corn Cob twisted violently on his seat, searching first with his eyes, his guts twisting in despair at the thought of being without his crutch. Not seeing the pipe he dove forward, leaning over the side of the boat to plunge his arms elbow deep into the water, his hands flailing about trying to grasp the precious pipe.

"Don't you know what you've done?" he wailed.

"Me?" said Fat Head. "You're the one muttering the dreaded *thing that shall not be named*. How dare you curse this ship with your foolishness?"

"It's out there, you know that! Oh, God, I need a pipe."

"You've had twenty this morning already. What you need is a good box around the ears."

"Where is it?"

"It's gone."

Something brushed Corn Cob's fingers. "Ah, here it is," he cried in triumph. His elation was quickly quenched by pure terror as he tried to grasp it.

But instead the thing tried to grasp him.

"Get back, you fool!" said Fat Head, grabbing Corn Cob by the scruff of his collar and dragging him back from the edge.

A mouth full of teeth opened up in the water like a portal leading to a damned abyss of pain. It snapped shut around the space Corn Cob's arms had been a split second earlier.

"Shark!" shouted Rat Teeth, not in alarm but triumph.

Corn Cob fell back stunned as the water before him churned to froth, the white wash masking the retreat of the shark like a cloud of smoke conjured by a stage magician doing a disappearing act.

"Th-the megalodon," he stuttered, his teeth chattering as if he'd been pulled from icy water. His worst fears had been realised. His eyeballs vibrated in their sockets, unable to focus on the face of the captain as he loomed over him, his fat head splitting into two and then four heads like a chimera born of myth.

Fat Head slapped him hard in the face, and the four heads snapped back into a single one, fat as ever and trembling with rage.

"Don't say that word on my ship!" he bellowed, his neck turning an angry red yet his face pale with barely masked fright. "It was a regular shark, you damned idiot, not some monstrous creature from the deep come to kill us."

"We're rich," said Rat Teeth, so drunk he hadn't considered anything beyond the fact that there were sharks in the water, and that meant money and more grog for him, perhaps enough for a year of lost time and dulled senses. "They've taken the bait after all."

"That one jumped the hooks," said Fat Head, trying to steady himself by focusing back on the work.

"No, but there's more out there," said Rat Teeth, pointing. The water around the ship was agitated, many small waves and eddying currents competing to swirl around the boat.

"God, but something has got them riled up." Fat Head hit the winch lever once more to drag more of the line in, praying and cursing under his breath. A shark emerged from the water, thrashing and fighting.

Corn Cob recoiled from it in terror. Fat Head laughed, his face flushing pink with relief. This shark was on the line, the hook pierced through its mouth.

"See, they're nothing but regular-sized sharks out there, not some damned fairy tale," said Fat Head.

Corn Cob brushed himself off and got to his feet, his breath shallow and frantic. He clutched his chest, where his heart still beat fast. He tried to slow his breathing but couldn't. Fear had its hooks in him. This wasn't helped by the look of bloodlust he saw in the eyes of one of his fellows as the shark was hauled to hang over the deck, its body wriggling violently to escape, jaw chomping in an attempt to free itself.

"There's killing to be done," said Rat Teeth, hefting a cudgel with a gleaming smile of small, sharp teeth. He handed Corn Cob a giant knife.

It felt cold and heavy in his hand as he closed his fingers around the grip, the sun catching the long blade with a brilliant flash of light. It was like a warning beacon going off right in Corn Cob's face. He nearly dropped the thing in fright, wanting to run away and get clear of the killing field. It wasn't the sharks but he who wouldn't see another dawn.

His whole body trembled. The knife seemed to vibrate and hum in his hands. He felt like he could hear it, buzzing in his ear, speaking to him, telling him he was going to die. He tried to shake his head to clear it, and it took him a long moment to realise the sound was Fat Head humming a tune in grim satisfaction, striding forward to inspect the shark. The captain ran a hand down its grey, slimy flank, the creature recoiling from his touch, knowing death was close and wanting to fight.

"No escape for you," sang Fat Head like a menacing lullaby, the words deep and resonant, striking Corn Cob in the bowels so that he too felt the fear the shark must have felt as it was abandoned by the sea and left to the tender mercies of the ruthless humans.

"Alright," said Fat Head, stepping back. "Put the thing out of its misery."

This call to action steeled Corn Cob, because, despite the implied murder to which he was to participate, it spoke of empathy and an end of suffering. He gripped the blade in his fist tightly so it would stop vibrating like a living thing. It became cold and inert as he braced himself, readying for the kill.

Rat Teeth was already bashing the shark's brains out with his cudgel and Corn Cob saw the transfixed, horrified eye of the shark as its skull cracked and its whole world started to fade. Still, it fought, though it didn't know how, its whole body tensing one moment and becoming a slick, writhing worm the next, corkscrewing about.

"Get into it, will you?" said Fat Head, and he stepped back in to steady the moving mass of still-living meat. When this didn't work, he hugged it like a boxing bag being worked over by a champion boxer, held it in place as Corn Cob felt a lightning jolt jab him through the base of the spine, goad him forward. Without his own volition, acting on some neurologically forced impulse, he lunged forward, stabbing with the knife. It sunk deep into the shark's neck with little resistance, and nothing happened until he withdrew the blade. A font of blood gushed forth as from a geyser, splattering across the front of his rubber overalls and making him look like the abattoir worker he was. Corn Cob made an odd squealing sound like a grotesquely fascinated child—or slaughtered pig—and stabbed again as the shark's eye stared at him in mortal terror, the pupil transfixed and glassy.

Another cut, more blood, the blade snagging in cartilage.

"Stop fretting at it and slit the poor thing's throat," said Fat Head, rocking with the tremors going through the shark as Rat Teeth maniacally kept bashing at its head, laughing with demented glee as if it were a piñata. "Will you piss off?" Fat Head said to the man, but this availed nothing, for Rat Teeth was having too much fun. Only Corn Cob could end this charade.

He buried the knife into the shark's neck and grabbed the handle with both hands. With a heaving gesture like the stroke of an oar through water, he pulled hard across the throat of the shark. The head folded back as if mounted on a hinge and the shark's insides opened up to the world in a stinking rush of pink gore. It tumbled onto the deck, striking like a wave and spreading out into a steaming pool of entrails which made all of them slip and slide on their feet.

"God, well that's one, and money in the bank, too," said Fat Head as he hefted the carcass from the hook. The shark dropped with a dead thud onto the deck to roll about in its own guts. "Let's hope the next one goes a bit more smoothly, eh?"

Rat Teeth looked at the shark as if he were going to continue beating it, but Corn Cob stepped his foot over to stand astride the thing, give it at least some dignity in death and protect it from the frantic horror show of Rat Teeth's tender mercies.

Truth be told, Corn Cob felt a spike of guilt at his own part in the killing, knowing it was neither merciful nor swift. The knife in his hand felt hot and heavy, like a lump of iron pulled from the forge, and he nearly dropped the thing. But Fat Head was working the winch, dragging in another length of line, and on it, another shark.

The fear Corn Cob felt made the heat in his hand rush to his head, there to fizzle and sizzle, take away any thoughts of mercy. He was ready to kill if only it meant his own survival. The knife flashed in front of him as he wove a defensive web around him, the play of light off the blade like the gossamer strands of a protective web.

"Save your energy," said Fat Head as the shark loomed over the deck. This one was even bigger than the first, but it was no megalodon. Corn Cob fought to slow his breath, knowing they had a long day ahead of them, many more sharks on the line. Soon the killing and the exertion would make him numb and weary. He tried to think of the money, but this weighed him down even more.

The second shark stared at him with the same moist eyes as the first, though this time he was more than ready to silence their mute accusation. But before Rat Teeth could brain the thing with his cudgel, the whole boat jerked violently down to one side as some colossal weight tugged on the line with the strength of a giant. The back end of the boat sunk towards the waterline, the surface of the sea churning to froth.

***

The three men were thrown from their feet, landing in a tangled mess of sharp hooks which jabbed into their flailing limbs as they cursed and wailed.

"I told you. I told you," said Corn Cob hysterically as he rolled about in watery blood, kicking his legs and pounding his fists on the deck.

"Fuck this, and fuck you too," said Fat Head, struggling like a beached whale.

Rat Teeth was the first to rise, jumping nimbly to his feet. He had his cudgel lifted defensively like a wooden cross used to ward off evil. Backing away towards the cabin, his face was drained of colour.

"Captain," he said, pointing with a bony finger. Fat Head turned, but Corn Cob just closed his eyes, not wanting to see what he knew would be there.

The still-living shark was off the hook.

***

The beast was furious, a great tear along the side of its mouth where it had ripped free of the hook. Wanting to get back into the water, it writhed on the deck like a cut snake, bending at the middle and bucking up and down. Its dorsal fin caught the sunlight with its glossy wetness, the sail of a ship in distress.

The shark thrashed back and forth, knocking aside hooks and tackle and getting tangled in the process. Its tail fin slashed the air frantically like an unskilled sword fighter waving their weapon about, impotent to cut itself free. This failing, it threw itself at the side of the boat in a bid to propel itself over the side and into the waiting sea, but only succeeded in bashing its nose painfully against wood several times.

It turned at bay as the three fishermen recovered, gaining their feet and arming themselves. Corn Cob gripped his knife uncertainly and Fat Head had found a long metal hook. Rat Teeth was hanging back, his club not a weapon for the moment, but a pointing stick.

"Get it, get it," he squeaked, huddled in the frame of the cabin door, ready to flee down below. Fat Head laughed derisively at him with dark mirth. Corn Cob thought Rat Teeth had the right idea and started edging away. Fat Head grabbed his arm and drew him tight to his side with a menacing growl, the sound like gravel crushed underfoot.

"You stick with me, mate," he said. Corn Cob could only gulp down the lump in his throat and nod, sweat beading his forehead.

The shark was going nuts. The grotesque presence of its slain mate seemed to add a level of horror as the live shark butted up against the dead one. Seeming to sense this was its fate too, it was easy to understand its desperate need for escape.

And it's not like things were going well for the crew either. The whole boat was lurching down towards the waterline now. Corn Cob looked at the straining line, taut and shivering, and then at the knife in his hand. He shook his head in answer to his silent question to himself and glanced at the wooden chest he'd sat on earlier.

"Don't you dare," said Fat Head, guessing his purpose. He gave him a shove away from the chest and towards the shark. Corn Cob nearly fell, sliding and stumbling on spilled guts. The mouth of the shark opened wide to meet him and he stared down into the gullet of the thing.

There he saw death.

***

A chomping chasm of blood and pain lined with row after row of razor sharp teeth. The gums of the shark were pink like gore, its gullet a black hole. Corn Cob visualised himself inside it, looking out, the mouth closing over his head, cutting him off from life.

Darkness prevailed.

***

"Get up, you stinking coward!" bellowed Fat Head in Corn Cob's ear. It was a loud foghorn, a slap to his consciousness, a warning bell going off.

Corn Cob shook his head, his vision blurry. He could hear screaming. For a moment he thought it was his own. There was terrible agony in that voice, though, and he felt no pain, so he dismissed the idea.

"I... I must have passed out," he said, his voice reed thin, barely audible over the shrieking he heard. It was accompanied by a tearing sound like cloth being torn.

"You fainted, you damned sissy," said Fat Head. The big man grabbed him under the armpits and hauled him up—or at least to a position which felt something like up. The deck beneath Corn Cob's feet was at a steep angle. His boots kicked air and the heels slid in slime, finding little purchase.

"What's happening?" muttered Corn Cob, his vision clearing enough that he saw blocky shapes moving frantically across each other—red, grey, and blue. He worked his eyelids mechanically with heavy blinks, and these abstract shapes slowly resolved into a horror show of gushing blood and flailing body parts against a backdrop of churning, foamy sea, revealing the source of the screaming.

Rat Teeth had fallen from the cabin as the stern of the boat had lurched down into the water.

Corn Cob swallowed hard.

"Straight into the waiting mouth of the shark," he said. The thought was too terrifying to contain it in his head, but as the words were set free in the air they had an even worse effect—on himself and the captain as well.

Fat Head abandoned him, making a dive for something more solid as the deck tilted down even more. His heavy weight landed against a metal pole with a grunt of expelled air. It was one of the outriggers, which was bent like a fishing pole bearing the load of a heavy catch. The line attached to it vibrated like a taut guitar string. On the other outrigger, the second line was slack, but it danced about and occasionally caught tight, making the outrigger snap back and forth like a whipping antennae. Corn Cob could see sharks circling in the water beyond the boat.

He let out a strangled cry of fear as he began to slide down the deck towards the terrible scene of Rat Teeth's gruesome end. With a spasm of his body he lurched to one side and grabbed hold of something boxy and hard, a jagged corner jabbing him in the ribs like an accusing finger, telling him he should have known better than to have got involved with these madmen, because now he was sure to be eaten by a shark.

Just like Rat Teeth.

The sight of the man's munching dismemberment in the jaws of the beast was terrible, too terrible for the mind to contemplate. Corn Cob's eyes slid over the details in an effort to block out the horror. Still, there was no ignoring the torturous soundscape of pitiful screams and the sawing bite of those rows of razor teeth, not to mention the liquid gagging noise of the shark gulping down chunks of Rat Teeth's flesh.

This auditory assault sliced through Corn Cob's soul. He wanted to give up, leave the world behind. It was all too much to handle anymore. But a face came to him in his mind, a woman's face. The look she gave him was soft and homely, reminding him of something worth living for. It forced him to go on. He smiled sadly for a moment, feeling a depth of longing he had never known, thinking he'd always come home to her, that there was no such terrible fate as this waiting for him each time he went out on the boat.

The face faded, replaced by Rat Teeth's agonised visage in its place, and Corn Cob's smile similarly morphed into a grimace.

He didn't want to die.

But the boat was going down, and there were sharks in the water.

***

Hell, there was a shark in the boat. But not for long, as the stern rail of the ship was fully submerged and the shark was able to thrash itself clear, dragging Rat Teeth off into the wider sea. Corn Cob heard the man emit one final gurgling scream before he went beneath the bloody, foaming waves, his life cut off now by a lack of air as much as by the shark eviscerating him.

"Drowning or being eaten by a shark, those are our options now," said Fat Head. He had the long hook in his hand. He was using it alternatively to fend off another shark snapping at his boot and to gain some purchase on the timbers of the cabin as he teetered on the brink of falling.

"Not if I have anything to do with it," said Corn Cob, trying to muster what courage he could, most of it supplied by the shimmering mirage of the woman's face, its outline still hazy but present in his mind like the echo of some shouted encouragement. He looked around for his knife, but he'd lost it at some point. His fingers dug into the wooden surface he clutched to in desperation. It was the big chest he'd sat on earlier. The fact that it was bolted to the deck had saved his life. His mind returned to his contingency plan—perhaps it could do so a second time.

Down below, in the water, was a frenzy of shark bodies, grey and slimy, the fins thrashing about like banners of an invading army, hungry for the blood of their enemies. They were bashing against each other in their eagerness to get to the warm bodies above, driven mad by the blood in the water from Rat Teeth's grim demise.

His body was long gone now, not even a scrap of rag floating on the water, with only a red smear on the surface to show he ever lived.

Corn Cob wanted more than anything to not share that fate.

"I want to live!" he shouted in defiance.

"So do I, you bloody mongrel," said Fat Head. He'd given up trying to use the hook to deter the shark—it wasn't doing any good. Instead he was kicking his attacker in the nose with his boot, trying to steer it towards Corn Cob, clinging to the chest. The ship lurched lower into the water, bringing man and shark into nail-bitingly close proximity.

"Don't fucking point that fucking shark my way," bellowed Corn Cob.

"Come on, you fucking bastard. What do you have to live for?" said Fat Head. He was augmenting his betrayal by using his hook to prod and jab at Corn Cob as if he were a sausage on a grill, some tender morsel to tickle the fancy of the hungry. Speaking to the sharks, he said, "Go on, you greedy mongrels. Feed on him, not me."

Corn Cob used one hand to swat away the hook, nearly losing his purchase on the wet, slippery chest with the other.

"We can both live if you just fuck off," he said to Fat Head, but the man was determined to sacrifice him in some vain effort to save himself. The hook caught in the fabric of Corn Cob's sodden woollen sweater and Fat Head beamed in triumph as he was able to drag the other man around, bringing him close to falling.

But this move cut both ways. Corn Cob wrapped one hand around a wad of the sweater, using it to grip the hook tight. The other held the edge of the chest by desperate fingertips as he dangled over the waiting sharks like a proffered piece of bait. The monstrous beasts snapped angrily at the air, their teeth clinking together like the bones of the dead. Using their tail fins to propel themselves into leaps, they took turns attempting to snatch at Corn Cob's legs. Their noses scraped his boots, filling him with terrified purpose. He tugged at the hook bridging him and the captain.

"Let go, you daft bugger. You'll drag me down with you," said Fat Head, realising the tables had turned. He tugged the hook violently as he fought his crewmate. He could have just let go of the thing, but there was a murderous glint in his eye and he seemed intent on feeding Corn Cob to the sharks.

"I want to go home," Corn Cob pleaded.

"And I don't?" said Fat Head.

"You don't even like your wife. You hate her. She hates you. At least let me go home to mine."

"You don't have a wife."

"We're married in our hearts."

Her face shone in Corn Cob's mind, radiant as an angel. Fat Head scoffed.

"You sentimental fool," he said, continuing the tug of war with the hook.

"They won't be satisfied with just me," said Corn Cob, trying one last time to reason with the man.

"Yeah, but you'll keep them busy for a moment," barked Fat Head, his eyes wide in terror, spit foaming at his lips.

Corn Cob knew there was nothing for it. It was either him or this oaf. He stopped pulling at the hook, and instead, he pushed. The change threw Fat Head off balance, perched precariously on the outrigger pole, and his vast bulk swayed back and forth. He dropped the hook, wind-milling his arms. Just when it looked like he might find his equilibrium, the boat shunted to the side, a heavy tug on the line in the water pulling it down. Fat

Head swayed forward, his big belly folding like kneaded dough. Then he arched back, his spine like a drawn bow.

He was going to fall anyway, but Corn Cob used the long-handled hook to give him one final shove, wanting to be certain in the knowledge he killed the man who had tried to kill him.

Fat Head tumbled backwards, flopping against the deck, vertical now like a wall, and bouncing off it.

Straight into the waiting mouths of the ravenous sharks below.

***

They tore Fat Head limb from limb, teeth like knives slicing and sawing at his flesh as he screamed in agony. His face was a mask of shocked disbelief—no one thought it would be them who ended up with such a grisly fate, and the mind rebelled against the notion.

But this wasn't the case for Corn Cob—he knew only too well he was next unless he did something drastic. And that something was what he should have done a long time ago, what he wanted to do when he first saw the line was overburdened. He'd not been the one who was so greedy or plain stupid enough to let this get to the point where they were the prey instead of the hunters. The sharks were now the ones who were harvesting their catch.

"And just so we could sell your carcasses to some other greedy, stupid idiot in another country to make shark fin soup!" he yelled at the sharks, annoyed with himself, and with Fat Head, but not with the sharks, who he knew were only dumb creatures trying to live. It didn't make it any easier to know they'd eat him all the same. He willed them to leave him alone. If they did he promised not to fish anymore and would never hurt another shark.

But the ravenous monsters weren't going anywhere. They were in a blood-frenzy, frantic and thrashing in their hurry to get their share among the writhing grey bodies and shaking fins of their fellows. With angry, chomping jaws they dismembered Fat Head, who was no longer screaming, his blood all outside his body, spreading in an expansive pool of red.

He was dead.

Where once there had been a living man, now there was only a floating mass of butchered flesh, bobbing in the water like a bloated sack of air, an inflated balloon in some aquatic sport, passed back and forth by unskilled athletes, bumping him with their pointed noses. All his limbs were torn off, leaving just tattered strings like party streamers. His bulbous head was engulfed by the yawning bite of one of the bigger sharks, disappearing in one gulp down its gullet as its guillotine jaws closed. Big chunks of torso were similarly chomped away, leaving cartoonish semi-circular bite marks in the remaining flesh.

Soon there wasn't much left of the big man. The grisly remains were periodically gnawed at, the last pieces worried free by sharks shaking their heads with jaws clamped on meat. Finally, there were only little pieces left, bobbing around like abandoned tennis balls in a pool. The big sharks looked like little fish now, nibbling at these tiny bits disinterestedly.

Corn Cob shook his head in horrified disbelief. With his hefty bulk Fat Head had been a huge meal for the sharks. Yet they weren't done. In fact, even more sharks had gathered around—maybe just arrived, or perhaps they shook themselves loose from the hooks.

There had to be something still hooked, though—the line attached to the outrigger remained taut and dragged heavily on the boat, taking it down into the water further with a heaving lurch that suggested a vast weight was on the other end.

If Corn Cob couldn't get that line loose, he'd have no hope. His feet dangled closer to the waiting jaws of the sharks as the boat continued to sink lower.

***

He flexed his grip on the wooden chest in grim determination, willing himself to at least take this last chance that fate had offered him. He was still alive, and though death was looming close now, here he had the means to do something about it, if only he was brave and skilled—fuck it, *lucky*—enough to pull it off.

The chest wasn't locked, and he needed to get inside it. That proved to be the easy half of the problem. As the boat tilted further and nearly capsized, pulled down by the weight on the line, the lid of the chest swung open like a door. He clung to it with both hands, frantic to maintain his hold but nearly thrown off by the swaying of the whole boat around him. The sharks saw him dangling above them like a tasty morsel and renewed their efforts, leaping up and snapping their jaws with a sound like knives being scraped together.

With a strength born of fear, Corn Cob pulled himself up, heaving his belly onto the top of the chest lid as it flapped about like a window shutter caught in the wind. The boat rocked, slamming the lid closed on a fold of his flesh, making him howl in pain and frustration.

"Just take me now," he said, rolling his eyes to the heavens. Seagulls circled overhead like vultures. Their shrill cries were like exhortations to either keep going or give up, he couldn't tell which. They were an echo of a confused voice inside his soul, and for a moment his grip slackened and he sunk down, ready to let go. But one thing the slamming of the chest lid on his stomach did was remind him of the pain which would accompany the jaws of the sharks snapping closed. The primal sensation, reinforced and made real through his vivid imagination, goaded him to action in a way reason never could.

A shark burst from the water, angled vertically as it shot up, and brushed his boot with its rubbery nose. This was enough to decide the matter. That touch was electric, like the spur of a zapping electric cattle prod. He sprung like a spring up onto the top of the chest. Sitting on the wooden chest, his legs swung alongside the lid. He rubbed his stomach to ease the pain there. It made him look as if he were a greedy boy, looking down hungrily on a prospective meal of shark, rather than the grim reality of the opposite. The black eyes of the sharks were fixed on him, their jaws biting the foamy water in anticipation of the feast to come.

"Not just yet," said Corn Cob, reaching down between his legs, rummaging around in the chest for the salvation he sought. Relief washed through his body as his hand gripped something hard and firm.

It was the axe.

***

The ship was sinking fast. The outrigger was bent in a U-shape, the attached line taut and humming, shaking with drops of water. Roles were now reversed, the boat the bait and the ocean had its mouth open to swallow it whole.

"That's not a regular shark on the line. Not even a hundred sharks could pull like that," said Corn Cob. Not that it *had* to be anything worse—a normal shark would do him in just as they had the rest of the crew—but his mind was delirious now with fear. It repeated a single word to him, over and over.

Megalodon.

The water rushed up at him as the boat was dragged down. The bubbling surface of the sea was festooned with frenzied sharks. He had not a moment to spare— adrenaline spiked him hard in the base of the brain, forcing his limbs to act. He was a puppet now, directed not by thoughts and reason, but by instinct and primal terror.

He jumped up onto the side of the chest, the boat vertical in the water. His arms swung to gain balance, but he had the weight of the axe to steady himself. It was a reassuring lump of wood and steel, something to ground him back in the reality of life and the prospect of survival. Riding the bucking boat with his seaman's legs, he swung the axe up over his head.

"I'll see you again," he cried, his eyes blurry with tears as he thought of his woman and home. He struck down with the axe, the heavy steel head colliding with the thrumming cord of the line.

It was like stroking the string of a giant guitar—rather than breaking, the blow rang a single note, piercing and clear. It was a ringing bell, a death knell. It was the sound of death coming for him.

Corn Cob cursed, but he didn't give up, hefting the axe once more. The water was boiling around him, the chest beneath his feet half submerged. A shark arced up and bit his foot, tearing through the gumboot, teeth slicing flesh. He screamed. The pain and terror ripped through his body like lightning, giving inhuman force to his next blow.

It hammered down. Strands of the taut line parted with a twang. They unravelled, coiled like pig's tails. But the line still held, its core straining but intact. Corn Cob gave a sob, saw the tattered strands of his shredded foot mirrored in the frayed line. One more blow was all it needed, but he didn't know if he had it in him. With the last of his reserves, his body pushing through the shock of pain and blood loss to give him a final, thin chance of surviving, he lifted the axe, hopping on one foot as the water rose to cover it. A shudder rippled up his spine to know he was now *in* the water with the sharks.

The beasts saw this and closed in for the kill. One lunged at him and he had no choice but to respond. As he swung the axe down he redirected his aim from the final, but now probably futile, blow he had for the line—the one which he hoped would sever the remaining strand and finally cut the stricken craft free of the monster on the other end.

Instead, he went for the closer threat, the one that made the most sense and which wasn't a phantom. This was a real shark, not some myth conjured up from the depths of the ocean, from the fathomless recesses of the human psyche. Here was an animal trying to eat him, and he had to defend himself or die.

The shark went for his foot. He went for it with the axe. The blow chomped into its body with a meaty thwack, swallowing the axe head whole, buried into cartilage and flesh. The stricken shark reared up like a performing dolphin on its tail fin and spun a jack-knife pirouette in its death throes. Corn Cob was nearly pulled from the chest such was his rigor mortis grip on the handle of the axe. But he was forced to let it go, the weapon stuck deep in the flesh of the creature.

With a quaking heart, Corn Cob watched as the dying shark swam away, the axe handle sticking up in the water, a marker for its grave—and his own, the weapon his only lifeline. He clenched his hands impotently, feeling their emptiness. The water was up to his waist now, and the sharks were circling.

The whole boat tipped over at a frightening angle like a cresting wave as a huge shudder ran along the frayed fishing line. Whatever was on the other end was impatient for its meal—or to escape. Corn Cob wailed, wishing he, too, could be free of the strand of fate which had him on its hook. He dropped down onto the chest, clinging to it with his arms and legs wrapped around it like a baby animal clutching its mother. He quaked, drenched with water, but not cold, his teeth chattering with terror.

The line sawed away at the foamy water, zigzagging back and forth like a dark beam of light scouring the surface of the sea. It scattered the sharks as it sliced about wildly. The boat shook like a tree in a storm— Corn Cob knew it must soon go over, completely capsize. That would be the end of him, and a relief it would be too. His overwhelmed mind saw it as a way out. He felt an icy surge of sensation wash over his body, tingling across his skin like fire as the adrenaline rioted in his blood. It was a confusing feeling, a call to action full of impotent contradiction, as he had nothing to do but wait for the end. It's not like jumping into the water would save him. If only he had been able to—

With a sound like a cracking whip the final strand of the line gave way.

**

Corn Cob was hurled as if by a catapult as the tension was released and the boat flexed. His whole world was nothing but rushing, tumbling confusion, his vision swirling into a blur as he was thrown end over end. He landed with a splash, the water's hard surface like the backhanded slap of a giant's palm. It knocked him unconscious for a second, and when his brain rebooted, his lungs flexed, drawing in not air but water.

His insides burned. He choked and gagged. Stars danced across his vision as his mind struggled for air that wasn't coming. Like a man tied up, seeking to be free, he kicked and convulsed his whole body. The water pressed down on him like soil thrown into a grave, heavy and cold. His movements were agonisingly slow compared to the sensory overload of his panicked state. But he struggled on, desperate to live, even if it were for only a few minutes more. His existence myopic, his mind sought only the oxygen it craved. The sharks were a forgotten phantom, haunting only his subconscious, lurking there, waiting to see if he'd first survive this suffocating gauntlet of water.

His limbs slowed even more, starved of the oxygen they needed to carry on, running on pure adrenaline and forlorn hope. Every cell in his body screamed for release from the torment, crying out to breathe. His blood boiled in his veins. Bubbles popped in his brain. Arteries seemed fit to burst like cracked plumbing pipes. Corn Cob had no more thoughts, and even the numb actions of his body were becoming sludgy, his flesh dissolving into immobile mush, floating like a jellyfish, taken with the current.

More stars flashed in his vision, closer this time, as if they were *inside* his eyes, seeking to explode outwards. The crushing pressure in his head was becoming unbearable and he started to black out. His body flexed in spasm, a death throe masquerading as one final spasm of hope in his desperate bid to live.

He broke the surface. The intensity of sensations in the open air—the brilliant light, the widening spaces, and the scourging wind—was like getting hit over the head with a plank. He nearly went under again, but his body was buoyant enough he flopped backwards, chest and head above the water, arms outstretched like a crucified criminal on a cross. His stomach heaved and he vomited up on himself, the briny bile sliding down his mouth and face. It burned his throat, which woke him up a bit. His mind told him that such sensations meant he was still alive, though he couldn't yet remember where he was, what had happened, so starved was his brain of oxygen.

He heaved himself forward, choking as his scoured lungs tried to rid themselves of the water that filled them like a pair of overflowing jugs. The liquid sloshed around inside him as his diaphragm heaved, coming out his mouth as if his body were an old-fashioned hand pump at a well. The lever of the pump was being worked by some uncaring god as they simultaneously brought him back to life and tortured him to death.

It was only when enough of this water was gone that he was finally able to suck in a few spluttering breaths. They were shallow and incomplete, insufficient to rouse him to full consciousness, but enough that automatic systems in his brain kicked in. They worked overtime to keep him afloat, his limbs flapping weakly, as they sought to desperately pump the bilges of his rotting hulk of a body.

The explosive stars which filled his vision weren't clearing, but they were coalescing into a single, brilliant star, stabbing him with many beams of light in its attempt to rouse him. He squinted, but it was little relief, as the beams were small and focused—they got in under his eyelids, through the filtering shield of his eyelashes. There seemed to be some type of message being conveyed in those beams of light, some unspeakable words from a higher power. Corn Cob let his eyes flutter open, fighting against the pain of doing so, and as he did, he saw a pair of golden gates open with them, swinging back and forth as if trying to decide whether to permit him entry to what lay beyond.

He saw a face there, smiling down at him. Its shape was rounded in the sun's silhouette, which now appeared dark as he was drawn back to reality by the memory of who the face belonged to. Not God, but his wife, and she was shutting the gates on him, telling him to go back, to live.

Corn Cob vomited again, all over her face, but she wasn't disgusted, though she did recede into the golden halo of light surrounding the dark orb at the centre of the closing gates. They slammed in his face, and with this act of cosmic denial and rejection, he was cut off, alone, floating in an ocean.

Floating in an ocean filled with sharks.

***

The remembrance of his situation—the realisation that the sharks were there in the water with him—should have left him cold. But he was too fed up, too ready to die to care. Not even the swarm of fins slashing the surface of the water like the masts of a flotilla of old ships filled him with much dread. All that was left was a fascination, wondering how, exactly, he would die, and which shark would be the one to take him. It was a grim exercise in imagination, and one his brain didn't have the energy to fill in with detailed, gory imagery. But he was aware the pain he felt now was nothing compared to what was coming.

Maybe it would have been better if he'd drowned.

He looked at the boat. Was there any hope there? No. The vessel was a stricken wreck, more a pile of flotsam and jetsam than a floating craft. Pieces of it drifted around a central shell—all that was left of the hull—now flipped upside down and looking like a cracked egg.

Corn Cob took in a deep breath, which was refreshing and innervating in an unpleasant way, stinging in his raw lungs yet giving him a last experience of life before the end.

The sharks were coming for him, having expanded their circle of searching for flesh. Now they were a swirling hurricane with him in the eye of the storm. Seen from the air, he was trapped, with a moat of death around him which he could not cross. It hemmed him in, made the end inevitable. But even if he could find the strength to swim, where would he go?

He glanced at the boat again. It was better than nothing. Shrugging would have taken too much energy, but it would have encapsulated how he felt as he took a few weak, half-hearted overarm strokes towards it. The sharks seemed to sense his movement, or worse, his intention to escape, but they didn't believe it possible any more than he did, and only closed their noose tighter, not yet cinching the knot around his neck and strangling the life from him.

He spat and coughed as tiny waves kicked up by their movements slapped him in the face. It was unpleasant, and each slap felt like the sea itself mocking him, calling him a fool. But he was drawing closer to the overturned boat—which on closer inspection was only half a boat, the other part having been torn off and sunk—and he dared hope he could at least escape the pain of being carved up by those rows of ravenous teeth. He felt the unpleasant memory of the sensation of slicing his skin with a cheese grater. What he faced would be many times worse than that.

Only ten more metres between him and the boat—he could make it if the sharks decided to remain dumb. He couldn't tell if he was bleeding, all he could taste and smell was salt, and any redness in the water was lost to his sore eyes. But he assumed the sharks could tell, and he cursed himself as one broke off from the others. Its fin carved through the water towards him. It was as if it smelled not his blood, but his fear. Or perhaps it could read his thoughts. He tried not to think about the beast bearing down on him, instead summoning the last of his reserves to push for the boat.

He needn't have bothered.

With a sound of cracking timbers and a whoosh of displaced water, a shark—one much more breathtakingly massive than any shark Corn Cob had dreamed possible—burst from the water and smashed the tattered remnants of the boat to kindling with a snapping crunch of its monstrous jaws. He briefly got a glimpse down the gaping abyss of its gullet before the bite closed like the jaws of a huge bear trap, the colossal teeth shining like steel in the sunshine.

Corn Cob's breath froze like ice in his throat, and a single word wheezed out of his lips involuntarily, chilled by his terror.

"Megalodon."

***

The scene of monstrous violence only lasted a second, all noise and fury, flashing before his senses. Just like that the boat—and the mother of all sharks—was gone, leaving only a sucking, gaping void in the water that dragged down everything in its wake. Corn Cob was pulled towards this swirling vortex, sliding down its sides as if it were a pit in the earth. He fully expected the huge shark to be at the bottom of this watery hole, its jaws open to swallow him like the pathetic morsel he was.

Instead the water swallowed him just as completely as it rushed into the space the passing of the megalodon had momentarily created. It was a crushing weight, and he had forgotten to take a breath. Even so, what air that was in his lungs was forced from him by the hammer blow, the water falling on him like an avalanche.

For a moment he couldn't see and his ears were roaring with the sound of rushing water—he was isolated, transported to another realm, one of chaotic confusion. He had no idea which direction was up or down.

He felt more than saw a wave of bubbles all around him, and he wondered briefly where they came from. But more important than where they came from was where they were going—up, towards the surface. He followed after them blindly, trying to ride their current because his limbs were now inert lumps of wood, impotently flailing in the water like broken paddles.

His sight returned, but whether this was a mercy or a curse, it wasn't easy to tell. At first all he saw was a gradient of light and colour, from deep, dark blue, through to a glistening turquoise. This oriented the scene before him, framed it at least with direction as the bubbles left him behind, abandoning him to his fate. He no longer had any strength to swim, or will to live. Now he only floated in the water, static as a hunk of food set in jelly, waiting to be devoured.

And there were plenty out there which wanted to eat him. The sharks resolved to his sight only as dark silhouettes. His sore eyes could make out no more detail, only moving shadows with jagged edges, fins cutting through water like blades through flesh, ready to carve him up.

But it was the sharks themselves which were being devoured, scooped up by a giant, dark hand and stuffed into an impossibly large mouth. At first he thought the shape was one of the sharks, right on top of him. But he had no depth perception, and as the small sharks disappeared into this larger silhouette he realised the creature he saw was further from him than he thought, and much, much bigger. It swooped back and forth, gulping down the sharks like a vacuum cleaner sucking up specks of dirt.

This went on for a long—or possibly a very short time, Corn Cob could no longer tell—until all the sharks were gone from the waters around him.

All except the megalodon, who had devoured the rest of its smaller kin and now turned to its final meal, the delicacy to savour last—human flesh.

The jaws of the monster opened like the gates to heaven through which he had before seen light, love, and his partner. Now they were replaced with the darkness of the gullet of the beast. Here was a hell which ironically wasn't a torture, only an end. It was an abyss to go down into and finally be at peace.

Death enveloped Corn Cob. There was no pain. His oxygen-starved brain didn't even register the bite of the sword-like teeth rending him apart as the megalodon swallowed his pathetic remains.

The monster swam on, unperturbed, a thoughtless killer, as it had for untold centuries. Having reminded all its lesser kin, and those who would hunt it, who was the real lord of the deep, it crossed the breadth of the Arafura Sea and entered the Gulf of Carpentaria in search of a mate.

2

The Tweed Shire, on the east coast of New South Wales, Australia, 2025

I awake in darkness. Memories swirl around me like a story I've told too many times. Am I bored of these repeated details, or are they made fresh with the retelling? It is much more than a dream, much less than history. It is an impression, a myth, able to change and grow each time I, or someone else, experiences it.

It is a life, even if it isn't real. Or, at least, it isn't real anymore. It is the past. And all of the past is a fiction, as much a stretch of the imagination as the future, both blurry, with vast gaps filled in with invention. And, since I am the one who invents these details and passes them off as truth, I am even more uncertain of the nature of reality than those I try to deceive with my confidence. But it is all a sham, an act. I'm an actor in a play, reading lines.

I can't even be sure what I experience now is real, let alone what someone else did in the past, or what I might do in the future. Is it all preordained? Is it all so blurry and forgotten even as it happens? Who is writing the lines I speak? Everything is sensory experiences—touch, sight, smell, taste, hearing, and so many other unnameable senses—with thoughts bouncing off them, each feeding back into the other in a loop. Who started the loop? Where does it end? Only in death, or perhaps with sleep—is there really a difference? Perhaps the end is another beginning, where we wake up in another realm.

It could be one just like the one I find myself in, with birds chirping the dominant feature for now. My eyes are heavy with sleep, and it takes an effort to prise them apart, each blink sticky, as if I'm reluctant to let go of what came before, whatever other reality I had left behind. I'm reluctant to think of it, and this is aided by the usual fog of forgetfulness which comes with waking, the dream fading as I get up, replaced by the mundane existence of the here and now—putting on shorts, feet on the cold tiles, opening the curtains to be greeted not by full day but a morning still shrouded by darkness.

Why am I awake this early?

The alarm on my phone goes off again. I hit snooze again, the motion automatic. I remember the factory, waiting for me in the future, the long day ahead with too many slow, dragging hours. My shoulders slump as I make for the door and the stairs beyond.

***

The steam rises to my face. There is heat in my hands. Thank God for coffee. My foggy mind ponders the wonder of youthful energy and where it is to save me from the rigours of existence. Despite being only nineteen I'm still tired from lifting weights at the gym last night, and that after another long shift at work. Yet here I am, up again, on again, riding a merry-go-round like everyone stuck in the nine to five, except at the factory it's seven to five—and those extra two hours are where death comes for even the young.

At least Mum is cooking me breakfast. The smell of bacon and eggs adds to the stirring elixir of the coffee to bring me to full consciousness. But this doesn't save me, only gives me enough energy to complain.

"I can't stand another day on the factory floor. I need to get out of there," I say to Mum as she slaps down the plate in annoyance, sick of my whinging.

"You've got to do your time, work your way up. That's what I did," she says in pinched tones, her lips squeezed together like a dog's bum.

"Work your way up? You did the factory for what, three weeks? Then the bloody admin assistant quit—"

"She got pregnant," Mum corrects me. "Just like I did with you, and what a blessing you turned out to be." She kisses the top of my head, turns her back on me, as if this will be the end of things. How little she knows me. Or, at least, she hopes thing were different. I speak back to her, literally to her back, as she keeps it turned towards me as she does the dishes.

"The admin got preggers and pissed off," I say, "and you just happened to have clerical experience, which you conveniently added to your resume last second, I might add."

"I worked the front desk at that vet's office."

"It was an animal shelter. They would have taken anyone. If one of the half-dead dogs could have worked the phones, they would have propped it up with a stick and put it to work."

"Don't talk about it like that. You don't know what it was like there. It was dreadful. The dogs weren't even sick. They weren't half-dead, just abandoned."

"They were dead when you lot were done with them," I mutter under my breath.

"What was that?" She pivots neatly on the ball of her foot, swoops in to try to scoop up my plate before I've finished eating. I hunch over it like a dog over its bowl, give a low growl I'm not proud of, but it comes out involuntarily.

"See? We all want to eat. And you're lucky you've got a home."

"I'll be out of here soon enough."

"And go where, exactly?"

"Go work on the fishing trawlers."

"And how's that going to happen?"

"I've got it lined up," I lie, as much to myself as to her.

"I worked hard to get you the job at the factory."

"No you bloody didn't. They're desperate for people because that factory is a great big, dusty arsehole."

"It's not that bad."

"Then why did you scurry out of there to the nice air conditioned office the first chance you got?"

"You know why. They needed someone to work the front desk."

"And you wanted out of the bloody hot shithole, right?"

"Hey, don't talk to your mother that way," says Mum's boyfriend Darrel, emphasising his point—or lamely trying to exert his authority—by banging the butts of his knife and fork on the table. It's less for my benefit than for Mum's. Like a trained dog, she responds to this petulant outburst as if it's the height of charm. She obediently puts his cooked breakfast in front of him, gives him the same kiss on the forehead she gave me. I scowl, feeling robbed of finite resources. I glare at him, and then at the plate in front of him as I finish my own without looking at it, barely registering the food going down. I'm still hungry, and my sore muscles strain, crying out for more which isn't coming. Not yet, anyway, the first break at the factory hours away. Even then it'll only be fifteen minutes to scoff down something, followed by more waiting, complaining all the while like a whinging hound at the backdoor, for lunch.

"What you looking so fucking glum about?" says Darrel, having already inhaled his food. He sits back in his chair like a reigning king in his throne, rubs the bulbous stomach bulging out from under his shirt. It's like a great mound of hairy flesh, leading up a hill to a weak, absent chest, all of it topped with a great grey slab of a head, unkempt like a mausoleum covered with lichen.

What the hell does Mum see in these bozos? I think, getting up.

"Some of us have to go to work, Darrel," I say.

"You know I'm off on account of my bum foot. You think it's easy living on the dole?"

"It's not just your foot that's a bum."

"I'll give you some of my hand if you like." Darrel makes a lazy attempt to get up and look threatening, but he can't get himself out of the chair before I'm up in his grill, looming over him, not as bulky maybe, but stronger than him, and he knows it. My bunched fist hangs like the sword of Damocles over his head. I'd let it fall if it wasn't for the tearful look my mother gives me.

"Damn it, Mum, don't cry," I say, lowering my fist.

Darrel glances over his shoulder with fat, wide eyes swivelling like radar dishes. "See what you've gone and done?" he says, managing to get up out of his chair to console Mum. She sinks into his embrace, wrapping herself in his arms like the co-dependent security blanket he's become, just like all the others since Dad left.

I scowl and turn, wipe my forehead to clear the bead of sweat gathered there, tickling me as it drops across the spot Mum had kissed, erasing the pleasant memory of love and care, replacing it with stress.

The factory is hardly going to make it any better.

***

Outside it is no longer dark. Dawn creeps over the horizon, seeming to set fire to the dry grass of the bush with its sweep of blazing orange light. There is a chill in the air and I hug my hoodie close to my hi-vis shirt and jog on the spot for a second, my shorts chafing against my thighs. I've got steel cap boots on—heavy like lead shackles—to complete the look of someone off to work on some construction site as an apprentice sparkie or carpenter. But I have no such prospects before me. I'm too dumb, lazy, or poorly motivated to get it together to apply for a trade. Instead, I'm stuck in the factory on minimum wage, working just as hard anyway, the hours longer than that of an apprenticeship, with crap conditions, no benefits, and, to top it off, dressed in the same clown clothes.

A beam of sunlight strikes my chest as I reach for my car door. It illuminates the fluorescent yellow of my shirt like the back of a poisonous frog. It feels like a warning, telling me to change directions. I swivel my head, listening to the birds of the bush, the stirring breeze in the trees, and in it I can hear the roar of the ocean, the waves striking the beach far away—yet not so far I couldn't drive there, spend the day at the beach instead of work. I shake my head to clear this illusion, to get rid of the desire for freedom. All it does is torment me.

Yet the ocean is out there, calling me.

I look back at the house. It's not a bad place—a roof over my head, Mum's cooking—but I can't live there anymore. Darrel has made it impossible. But beyond that, I've my own head to deal with. The rushing roar of the ocean persists in my ears, filling my skull with pressure and noise. I squeeze my eyes shut and clench my teeth, wanting it to be over, knowing it won't let me be.

Not until I'm out of here.

***

I slam my foot down, skid the car on the gravel in petulant defiance and swerve out of the driveway. In my head I go over and over the conversation with Darrel, thinking only now of good comebacks and insults. I wish I could remember them later to spit them in his face, but I won't—I have a plan in place to forget it all anyway.

The road is long and winding, houses hidden up concealed driveways, mere glimpses through trees. There are few other cars on the road, but I get stuck behind a tractor. I curse the driver, tap my left foot impatiently. I feel a hot mass in my hip pocket and I want to set it—and me—on fire. Jangling nerves shoot up and down my spine, spread across my skin like a network of burning spider webs.

I put my foot down. The engine roars in defiance and then sputters in protest. The road slides beneath me and the bush gives way to semi-tropical rainforest as I skirt closer to the coast, closer to work. It's a fine art, finding a place to stop on the way, not too far from my destination, yet with enough of a drive after to recover from the smack to the brain.

Here's my good spot, but it's no good today. There's someone pulled over there already. They're not there for the same reason as me, instead maybe engine trouble, or checking maps on their phone. I blast them an angry honk with my horn as I pass and see their head strike the roof. I don't look back.

The trees spread out into the patches, fleeing, as if they, too, are afraid of me. I'm afraid of myself. I need out of here and out of my head. The scenery changes with this mood, flattens, the road straightens. I can go faster. There are fields. The cows don't look idyllic to me, not peaceful. Their splotchy hides are like ink blotches a psychologist shows me, asks me what I see in them. Mostly I see sex and, strangely, gates. Maybe they're the same thing.

The cows look up as I speed past, munching their grass. I feel the lump in my pocket shift. There's nothing for it. I wouldn't normally stop here, not in the open. But even though there are cars passing occasionally, they're all country people, no cops out here, and they don't care what I'm doing.

But Mum does have to pass this way to work as well. I don't want her to see me, to catch me. That's the whole point of this elaborate exercise. Otherwise I'd do this at home.

I shrug, not wanting to hear any more protests. I need excuses, reasons to let this happen. She'll be a while, I tell myself. And she will. The office starts two hours after the rest of us, at a humane hour for some reason. I haul over into the gravel on the side of the road. There are mountains in the distance and sugar cane fields butting up against the cow pastures. All of it mixes into a blurred palette of greens and yellows that feels so threatening now but will soon be welcoming, a homecoming to a state of mind I crave.

I pull the weed out of my pocket. I feel better already, a psychological phantasm preluding the coming relief. Reaching for a pouch of tobacco in the centre console— not even Mum can say anything about this, she and Darrel smoke like chimneys—I open it up and rummage around for the papers and lighter. The lighter is located, but growing drama jangles in my blood as I can't find the papers.

"Don't tell me I used them all," I say, but know this isn't true as I fish my fingers ever more violently through the brown strands of tobacco. "Bloody Darrel, he hasn't even left me one. And I swear there's less chop in here than before. I'll gut him. Probably gave half to Mum and all, claiming he bought his own with his damn dole."

Pounding the steering wheel does little to help besides vent some of my frustration and anger. I shake my head, grind my teeth. The weed is right there before me, but I have no way of smoking it. So near and yet so far away—and the clock is ticking, the factory shift looming, a full ten hours of purgatory with no relief. I can't accept it.

In a panic, I sort through the junk in the centre console, praying for a single loose paper to roll the joint I need to get through. There's a receipt in there from the petrol station. Will it do in a pinch? I wish I had a scrap of newspaper at least. Placing the weed and tobacco reverently on the passenger seat, I begin my deep search of the car, underneath and down the sides of the backseat, in the boot, the doors. Finally, in utter despair and desperation, I go to the glove box. I've been avoiding it, as I never put my smokes or anything useful in there, just years old rego papers and insurance slips, stacked up like a loser's filing cabinet. Popping it open, the paperwork floods out in an avalanche. I let out an exasperated groan, but I catch sight of a flash of colour—yellow or maybe brown—among the white. This gives me a spike of hope, born of some subconscious memory.

I have to resist the urge to gather up all the papers and dump them on the side of the road—they do have my name and address on them after all. Instead, I dig through them like the garbage heap they represent, now mixed with the more regular rubbish—paper cups, plastic takeaway containers, and other miscellaneous nonsense—that lives permanently in the footwell of the passenger seat.

Seeing the flash of brownish yellow again I snatch at it like a life preserver—I'm drowning here, sweat washing my face. I realise I'm panting hard, my lungs tight. My hand closes around the object. It feels heavy like fate in my clenched fist, though it is small and light. Lifting my hand close to my face, my fingers open like the petals of a blooming flower to reveal what I have caught.

It is a corn cob pipe.

***

The flame from the lighter is so close to my face I feel the heat tickle the tip of my nose. It flickers like a Promethean torch before my moist, glistening eyes, promising some type of knowledge if not wisdom. This is an illusion, perhaps, but real for now, as it is a relief from regular life and a doorway to some other type of existence. I will learn something, or forget something, and either way, the burden of who I am will be lifted for a time.

I try not to think of where the corn cob pipe has come from, who it belonged to, only that it is filled with weed mixed with shredded tobacco. The fire touches the ground up drug. Green and brown burns bright orange-red as I suck in. The smoke is invisible, internal. It shoots along the stem of the pipe, tumbles down my fleshy throat chimney, swirls in my lungs which pump like a bellows, the membranous walls strong yet delicate, absorbing and pulsing as they push and pull on the macro and micro scale simultaneously.

My sponge brain goes tense as I hold my breath for a second, then release. The effects are immediate. My vision turns grey and fuzzy, eyes dry and red as the smoke fills the car, expelled from the flared nostrils of a dragon. I unconsciously crack a window and it flows out like blood from a wound.

The sun is slashing its sword across the horizon. I squint as it rakes across my eyes. The horizon is a series of mountains, now with their tops cut off. I can see the plateau of Springbrook from here. It is flat like a table. I momentarily think of blowing off work, escaping up into the Gold Coast hinterlands for the day, exploring the rainforests and waterfalls. They have plants up on the plateau that exist nowhere else in the world, the area cut off from the outside by a ring of cliffs like the fortifications of a castle. Thousands of years of isolation have inevitably led to novelty and uniqueness—I wonder if I was born there, the magic of the soil in my blood. But am I really so different from others? I'm nothing special. The tree ferns up there grow over ten metres tall. They are fed by magic in that secret place and only allow a few precious souls to witness their quivering heights. Just like me they yearn to go beyond the canopy made by ancient trees, fanning out overhead, filtering the sun's light. They, too, want to witness the pure, undiluted beams of energy which might illuminate the soul and promote growth to a new level.

I laugh, breathe in again—more smoke, more escape, visiting the place in my mind. I zoom out of the treeline, across the lips of the roaring waterfalls, and plunge into the cool pools below. I glide along the zigzagging trails, hear the whir of insects, the calls of the birds. This is peace, even if it is momentary. There has to be some end of the trail, some place I turn back, return to what came before. I witness a phantom foot hover over a coiled snake—red belly, black back. The scales catch the light like a threat which pulses along its writhing length. It hisses menacingly. I back away from this memory—I'm pretty sure this actually happened?—and take the trail back the way I have come. Moving like smoky air, I rush slowly across the abyss of the pale morning sky back to my car with its cracked window, my brain sliding through the gap smoothly to re-enter my body with a jolt of surprise and dislocation.

I look around, bleary and content, smiling like an idiot, everything momentarily forgotten, even if it never really could be. Memories stick in my heart even if they have fled my mind—there is a thread of a looming danger boiling in my blood, a remnant of that snake. I see it still, its long body coiled into my mouth. I snatch at it in panic, throw it across the car. The corn cob pipe rattles against the passenger window, falls back in among the random assortment of paper files from which it came. The ashes of the burnt weed tumbles loose like the remains of a tiny cremated body, consumed in some type of pagan rite.

I see in them the spectre of an ancestor. They are calling out for help, already dead but not wanting to be dead. The voice is like a familiar song from long ago, wafting on a breeze. In the air the message carries loosely, with little detail, only emotive feeling—the plea so strong I remember whose pipe this is. A face is conjured up from an old photo, with no name attached, just a label—great-grandfather. Mum pointed him out in a family album, the pages yellowed with age, the protective plastic tacky and reflective. The corn cob pipe had been in his mouth in the faded picture. He was standing on a pier, a giant shark suspended vertically by his side, hanging dead from a hook on a scaffold. Pride beamed from him like the sun, shadowy defeat from the shark, but this felt wrong somehow. This was no final victory.

There were two other men in the picture, but I know nothing about them. They seemed smoky and blurred, obscured by the breath of my ancestor. All that is visible in my memory is the rat-like teeth of one and the gargantuan fat head of the other. Further details I have to make up for myself. They are like cartoons, and my great-grandfather is no better really. Mum has a story she tells about him, about how he died. I don't know if it is true.

I look at the corn cob pipe in the footwell of the passenger seat. I know it can't be the same one, surely—that was lost at sea, even in the story. It stares at me like a blank, black fish eye. My vision rushes down into this dark hole at the centre of the pipe as if I were being swallowed down the gullet of a monster. There I die, not in pain, floating in a purgatory for a time, waiting to be released from my prison.

Waiting to live again in someone else's memory.

***

Chomp, chomp, chomp.

It is like being eaten in reverse, a portion of the body pinched off and regurgitated as the sharp teeth bite down. I hear a high-pitched screaming. It is not my own, but it rings in my ears, infects my blood.

Blood...

It greases the grinding, chewing gears of the beast as the guillotine jaws close once more. A conveyor belt is waiting to catch the corpse pieces, carry the victim off to its coffin. They are rammed rather than placed in this box, the doors of life and light slamming shut as the lid closes.

Then it's into a mass grave, the cardboard coffins packed in vertically to save space. It is my job to place them there. I am just following orders.

This is the factory. It is a hell on earth.

The screaming stops. I pause in my macabre duties. For a while there are no boxes coming down the line. Bleary eyed, I look at the clock above the opposite workstation. It says quarter past seven. There is still most of the shift left to go. I've only been here fifteen minutes.

Ten minutes. You were five minutes late, remember?

The thought is my own voice in my mind, but it feels like someone else's, admonishing me. I've had enough of this place already. I need to get out of here, get on a boat. The supervisor chewed me out for being late. I can feel the stinging bite marks of their mastication on my arse. Their mouth never stops moving—they're still telling me off now, or maybe yelling orders from across the factory floor, not targeted at me, more a general spray of petulant authority being projectile vomited across all us grunts. But it's too early for such things, and I'm too high. I float far away, willing to sell my body but not my mind. Not that I have any thoughts, only sensations—the beaming bright lights overhead are like a brutal sun, burning into my eyes, searing my skin. I close my eyes and pretend I'm on the boat in the midday heat.

There, in the bright darkness, I see a shark's mouth open wide to consume me.

The screaming begins again. For a second I fear it is my own. I gulp down a lump in my throat to prove it isn't. The lump sears my insides like a molten rock. I feel like I can see this burning ball of lava in a flash of brilliant light as I reawaken to reality. It's just the lights overhead slapping my senses around once more to remind me of where I am.

Wide eyed, with sweat pouring down my face, I look down the line of machines. The conveyor belt needs lubricating—the wheels squeal like pigs being led to the slaughter. The metal blade stomps down—an executioner's axe to end their lives. The screaming continues. More bodies come down the line—sealed up in their little plastic body bags, I can't see their contents but I suspect it's some type of food, a dead corpse made from some plant or another, chopped up finely by the spinning blades of a machine. These packets are folded up into their cardboard coffin boxes by yet another machine. The metal arms twist and fold, chugging like the pistons of a train. They shove the boxes along like prisoners goaded by brutal guards.

I see all this at one step removed, kept at a distance by the clear plastic safety guards surrounding the machines. It is a brutal reality television show I watch as if through a fishbowl, living a vicarious life, not understanding how the machine works. The mechanical pieces swim about with a mind of their own like curious fish, seemingly unconnected to each other, their journeys random, guided not by pattern but instinct. Even though I can see all the moving parts of the machine, see its skeleton bones supported by rubber tendons, I can make no sense of the guiding force behind it all. It is a mysterious mythology to my untrained eye, something to provoke superstitious dread and loathing of the alien.

The god of electricity and the demon of engineering have their way with the packets as they pump through the emaciated inhuman structure of the machine like shits through an intestine. I feel my own bowels stirring, and for a moment I believe I'm the machine here, repetitively grabbing the cardboard boxes as they are shat from the sphincter of the machine.

I look around for the supervisor. They are no longer yelling, no longer even present. They have evaporated like mist, leaving me chained to my machine, no hope of a toilet break. Am I the prisoner here? I glance at the door of the factory, wondering if I can actually leave. I know I can't, not yet. Looking at the clock, it's only been five more minutes. With growing panic, I glance back at the packing machine. The boxes are coming for me, no longer prisoners themselves, they burst free of their metal and plastic cage. Tumbling down the sluice they seem all too ready to do violence upon me with their mass assault. My back already aches, my feet feel flat and tingle with a burning numbness which spreads across the soles like a wildfire. The heat creeps up the back of my legs. I know that when it touches the base of my spine it will light this bony fuse, sending a sparkling signal all the way up to the powder keg of my brain, setting off an explosive reaction I will not be able to contain. I fight against it, frantically throwing water on it. But it's just a matter of time. I can't stay here forever, can't contain the eruption which seems inbuilt within my being.

I glance at the door again. Next to it is a fire alarm. It seems reasonable to pull it. There is a fire after all. Though, glancing around at the faces of the other workers, you would not guess it was the case. They look bored, and I want to yell a warning to them. Somehow I contain myself, pick up another box. It feels hot to the touch. I drop it. It joins the other discarded ones on the floor. They'll all eventually be scooped up and put back to work, the same as I have been. No loose ends here, nothing useless, though I sure as hell feel useless, marking time, waiting to get out.

I try to take a deep breath, knowing it's the only way to cope. It's going to keep on like this all day, ten hours stretching out ahead of me like a wide black hole which swallows all light. I grind my teeth and place another small box into a larger box. When it contains six of these I push the whole package down the line onto yet another conveyor belt. With a rending tear like flesh torn apart by jagged teeth, the sticky tape machine seals up the flaps of the wound it itself has made. It all feels so futile. More boxes, endless boxes. Where are they all going?

The clock is my enemy—it takes slow steps forward, second by second, creeping up on me like a grim shadow, hungry for my blood. I look away, knowing I shouldn't watch it. But even concentrating on the boxes—now overwhelming me, they never stop coming—is just another marker of time, a way of counting progress as one after another packet of six is shoved down the line. A worker takes these off the far end of the conveyor and stacks them on a pallet like stiffened dead bodies, ready to be taken somewhere far away and consumed by some faceless monster.

I close my eyes and see the open jaws of the shark, waiting to devour me, because, to it, I am nothing but food.

***

"I don't know about you, but I'm getting hungry," says a man's voice.

I open my eyes, a single blink, but the clock reads ten o'clock. Somehow, mercifully, time has passed and we're approaching morning tea break. I nod mutely at the man at the opposite workstation, his face resolving only slowly into recognisable features. His name is Sam, and he's fifteen or more years older than me. He smiles, his mouth and chin encased with a gossamer blue beard net so he looks like some bizarre Arabian princess. A similar hair net on his head makes him simultaneously resemble a hallucinogenic mushroom. They clash wildly with his fluorescent orange shirt, adding to the exotic psychedelic vibe so incongruous with this place of mundane work. I know I look just as ridiculous. We all do. It's not an endearing part of the job.

Sam is packing similar boxes to the ones I'm working with, only white rather than black. His workstation is also near identical, but facing the other way to my own. It's like he's living some mirrored, inverse image version of my life. The bored, tired look on his face contrasts with the wired panic I feel. I can't remember working all this time and I assume the boxes have piled up on the floor, back up the conveyor belt, clogging the packer. It's going to be a mess. I'm in trouble, the shouted voice of the supervisor already echoing in my mind.

Looking down, my hands move automatically like programmed machines. Glancing left and right, I see the little boxes coming towards me in one direction, the bigger boxes containing them going off in the other. In the middle is a synthesis of the two I have performed without conscious effort, hundreds of little boxes packed into bigger boxes, on into infinity like a set of Russian dolls nestled one in the other, like this is a productive use of anyone's time rather than an exercise in futility. I find myself hating whoever is buying these boxes and wish they would stop. The whole thing, the chain of production in which I am a single link, has happened in spite of me, not because of me. I didn't even need to be here for it. Luckily, due to the drugs, I haven't been. Not so lucky, they're wearing off and there's still a lot of the day left.

My stomach growls, a call to the wild. It is a return to baser nature and a drop in level from the lofty oblivion of drugs, back to the earthy realm of survival. It demands I get out of here, sustain myself with food, but, in my weakness, it also goads me to keep running once I get out the door, and never stop until I hit the ocean. Even then, I won't stop—a ship will come and carry me to some faraway land where I don't have any problems. I feel the pull towards the vortex that is the hole in the pipe waiting for me in the glove box of my car. I break out in a sweat as the fear of withdrawals takes a hold of me.

"Yeah, I sure could use something," I say to Sam. He nods and winks like he knows what I'm actually talking about. His eyes have a searching, piercing quality, and seem to read the thoughts in my head, or, much worse, project his own into the blank slate of my mind.

I shake my head as if to deny this, but don't dare think anything more for fear he will find me out. The weed has taken a bad turn, switching deftly to paranoia. The supervisor stalks like a prison guard, watching for any clues the prisoners are going to riot or escape. I feel the edge of violence in their stare, but maybe I'm imagining it. They stab their finger at people like a shiv, and one by one, these people fall down, or fall out, like soldiers dismissed from parade, their bodies folding into themselves as they dissolve into the walls or through doors.

"You and Sam are on second break," the supervisor says to me when I have been spared this summary execution. But it is only a stay of sentence, a delay, and one I find I don't welcome. Neither does Sam.

"Damn it, we're stuck here until the others get back," he says.

All I can do is nod, not understanding, the hands of the clock slowly shifting around to point at me, accuse me of something. I feel sure time will reveal my true nature. They will see through my façade and I'll be fired.

But would that be a bad thing? Then I will finally be free of this place.

***

"Okay, you two can go on break now," says the supervisor. "We're changing the packets to a new run, so take these last few spares over to the office." She hands me three or four boxes, the colour on the front indicating the flavour. When I get back, the whole place will have a different scent, the boxes will look different, and I won't be high anymore. Everything will be changed. Time will be the enemy and it will no longer go fast, but slowly, like poured molasses.

I flow out of the factory just as slowly. Sam is quick. He's heading for the toilets and then to the veranda where we have our break. He has needs to see to. I take the boxes to the office, forgetting who will be there until I turn the doorknob.

Walking into the air conditioned office space is almost traumatic. It reminds me of everything we don't have in the way of comfort in the factory. I see chairs behind a desk and suddenly want—need—to sit down, my legs and feet hurting now the drugs have abandoned me.

In one of the seats is Mum. My insides flip as she turns towards me. My eyeballs shudder in their socket in fear as her eyes lock onto mine. I think she's sure to expose me to the bosses and see me fired. Instead, she smiles, welcomes me. Thankfully she doesn't do anything more affectionate—there are no kisses on the forehead, no hot meals. I pass her the spare boxes for the mailroom, free samples they'll send out to try to get more shops to carry the product. She thanks me, looks at me a little askew, and I leave. It is only when I'm outside I realise I should have said something, anything. It would have been far less suspicious. I thought my mouth would betray me, and it has by keeping shut. I sulk off to the veranda, feeling defeated, with my whole body deflating as the drugs take away their bracing support.

***

My knees are knocking as I walk up the three steps onto the veranda. Everyone else has already had their break, except for Sam and one other man. Sam sees the state of me, senses I'm in need. He puts down his sandwich and gets up from his seat at the break table.

"You alright there, Michael?" he asks me. I hear my name as if for the first time. It burns through the last remnants of fog clouding my perception. Reality resolves a little bit more, and I feel Sam's guiding hand on my shoulder, leading me towards a seat. I weakly try to resist, but he has control of me, steering me like a rudder.

At the table is the third guy on break. He has a jar of minced garlic and a big spoon. There is sweat absolutely pouring down his bald head and fleshy face. He nods at me, smiles. His teeth are blunt spades, dumb herbivore's teeth. The spoon in his hand swoops down to scoop up a load of minced garlic, lifting it to his mouth. He shovels it in, the face flexing like a rubber glove as he eats. I recoil from this bizarre and disgusting sight. The mouth opens and closes, his pink tongue flashing grotesquely, smeared with minced garlic. I try to veer away, set my own course, but Sam's hand is strong and leads me on.

"You look a bit worse for wear, mate," he says to me. The words seem to be whispered into my ear, as if they're spoken just for me, like I'm receiving instructions and the only reason that I am worse for wear is because he tells me so.

"You need to get out of here," he continues, yet guides me on towards a seat. The hand becomes heavy as an anchor, mooring me to the spot. I plonk down. My mind tries to escape, wants to escape, back into the obscuring fog, but it is nowhere to be found on the sunny day. Birds are singing in the trees, the leaves emerald green, and beyond a lawn is the plantation with its cash crop we're all here to harvest, process, and pack. My body doesn't—can't—move. I imagine running away, but I don't. Instead, I sit there, even as the heavy hand is lifted and Sam takes his own seat opposite mine. He watches me closely as he munches on his sandwich. I see my own flesh being devoured in each bite, even though Sam is a vegetarian. A burst of ripe tomato—it looks like blood as it runs down his chin. His eyes bore into me as if I'm prey, or perhaps, more accurately, bait on the end of a line and he's waiting to see what he'll catch.

I look away, but the sight of the other man is no less comforting. The garlic goes in as if it were coal fed into the furnace of a boiler room. It seems to power this giant man, produce such heat as to make him melt. He wipes the sweat from the spongy folds of his forehead and offers me the same hand to shake.

"I'm Roger," he says. I take his hand even though I don't want to. The palm is sweaty, and its fleshy mass enfolds my own like the clammy embrace of a fish. Roger stinks too, the garlic soaking through his pores, washing over me in hot waves from his open mouth. He's still speaking. "I'm new here, started yesterday. Have you worked here long?"

"No," I say. It's all I manage.

"Michael has only been with us a few weeks," says Sam. He puts down his sandwich and juts his chin in my direction like a knife. It still oozes with tomato blood. "His mum is one of the office people."

"Oh," says Roger around more garlic, "which one?"

Sam says her name. It disgusts me to hear him say it. I want to reach into his mouth and pull her name from his throat, but I'm afraid he'll bite me, take my hand off. I look down at my hand on the table. It's shaking.

"Look, mate," says Sam. "If you're not feeling well, you can ask the supervisor to go home. There's no shame in it or anything, happens all the time."

I desperately want to leave.

"I need the money," I say instead.

"Don't we all," says Roger.

"How much does that half kilo of home brand minced garlic set you back?" Sam asks him, wiping his chin and looking a lot less ominous for it.

"Can't put a price on health," says Roger with a rancid belch. "But if you must know, two buck thirty."

Sam grimaces. "You think that's a healthy meal?"

"It gets the adrenal glands going."

My blood is storming in my temple, pounding my ears with each thudding pulse. My eyes dart about. I want to jump over the railing, run into the fields. First, I'll hit up my car, though, grab my weed, tobacco, and…

I break out in a cold sweat.

…the corn cob pipe.

I shudder, not wanting the terrible visions to return, yet no more desirous to stay here in reality with these two freaks.

"I might tell the supervisor I'm not feeling well," I say, nodding slowly. Sam is also nodding, and I can't tell if I'm mirroring him, or him me. The decision doesn't feel like my own—I'm driven to it by external forces.

"Yeah, it's for the best. Go home, rest up, come back tomorrow," he says.

I'm not coming back tomorrow, I think. *I'm never coming back.*

The blood roars in my ears like the waves of the ocean, as if I'm holding a seashell to them. It is a siren song, piercing and painful even as it seduces me. I picture myself on a boat with the sea all about me, the open air above. There is an illusion of limitless freedom.

But there's something in the water, making sure I can't leave the boat. Suddenly the boat is small, and I'm trapped.

Trapped.

I breathe shallowly, clutching my chest.

"Are you having a panic attack?" asks Sam.

I nod frantically.

"Just go home. I'll tell the supervisor you were throwing up or something and had to rush off," he says. Roger lifts his eyebrows but says nothing.

I'm up out of the seat and running, a line cast into the sea of the future. Sam watches me from the shore of the veranda. The fisherman's reel is in his hands but I can't see the invisible strand that ties me to him. I'm the bait, dangled out here to catch something much bigger. But

I'm caught already, the pipe has me. I go to it like a lover. It promises everything will be alright.

Roger frowns at me through the windshield as I start the car, throwing it into reverse. I back out of the car space, and when I look back to the veranda, he's shaking his head sadly, still gobbling down garlic, as if that's the answer to all life's ills. I can smell the fragrance of the weed in my hot car and can't help but feel something similar towards my drug of choice. I wonder how far down the street I'll have to go before I can pull over and smoke. I pop open the glove box and check the corn cob pipe is still there. The dirty brown hole at its centre winks at me like a puckering sphincter lined with shit. The smell of weed is replaced with the rancid stench of pipe tar.

I wind down my window, glance at Sam, seeking some type of solace from him, some comforting words. But he has his head down, a pen in his hand. There is a writing pad on the table in front of him. He's taking notes for some reason, as if what has happened is nothing but a story for him to record for later use.

I stomp my foot down on the pedal in disgust, my tires throwing up gravel as I speed out of there, no longer looking back. I'm looking forward, trying to find any port in a storm, a place to park and escape this agony of existence.

***

I am awakened by the sound of a door slamming. My eyes open with a snap, but I find they won't open all the way. Half-shuttered, with eyelashes filtering my sight like prison bars, I look around blearily. I don't know where I am. It's a room, but I can't orientate myself within it. It's gloomy, curtains drawn, the features of the room vague. I rearrange them in my imagination, trying to decipher what each looming shape means, just shadows on shadows—furniture, clothes, posters, television, all of them dark outlines against a grey background.

The one thing I can be sure of is that the surface beneath me is soft, which is at first comforting. But I'm in the sticky molasses of waking after a bender, and the soft cushioning of what I realise is a bed is cloying and sweaty, grabbing at me with soft yet firm hands of decadence, pinning me in place with their promises of sickly sweetness and everlasting comfort.

But such a thing is impossible. I can't stay here forever, as much as I want to.

Another slamming door—it is like a box around the ears, an admonishment for a crime I don't know I've committed. Perhaps it is the sin of simply existing.

"Michael!"

It's Mum's voice, muffled by doors which open and close, making her call echo and warble with anger and indignation. She's coming for me, bursting through the barricades I have erected. I sit up in bed. This is my room, the overall topography familiar through smoky lenses, everything blurred slightly as I blink. Vague silhouettes become possessions of mine, gathered over my short life, now rotting like a heap of garbage I need to cast off in my need to be reborn. Something has to sweep them all away, I can't do it myself. And that something is coming.

She bursts in like a storm wind, the door snapping open like the jaws of a monster. Of course I forgot to lock it.

"You got yourself fired!" Mum shrieks.

"Huh?" is all I manage. I can't remember even having a job.

"Sam came into the office, told the managers you were sick, which was all well and good, but I knew something wasn't right."

"Oh, the factory," I say with dawning realisation. "I got fired?"

"I got you that job and you blow it right away. You know how that looks? You know how that reflects on me? I need my job."

"I'm not feeling well. Can you come back later?"

"Later? There's no fucking later, Michael."

"I'm sleepy."

"That's because you're high. The room reeks of it."

"Bullshit."

"No? There's weed right there on the table by your bed."

"Michael has weed?" says Darrel, popping his head through the door like an inquisitive child.

"Not now, Darrel," snaps Mum over her shoulder.

"What's the big deal? You smoke too."

"Shut up, Daz!"

"Hypocrite," I say, flopping down on my bed. My head is turned towards the bowl of weed on the table. "Maybe you could get out now? I need to do some stuff."

"Me? This is my house. You're the one who's going to get out."

"What?"

"You need a good shove. You said you were going to go work the fishing boats. Well, best of luck to you. See if they put up with your nonsense."

Darrel laughs. "They're going to eat him alive."

I sit up straight in bed as if I've been electrocuted. "What did you fucking say?"

"Uh," says Darrel uncertainly, edging back behind the doorframe. "I said they're going to eat you alive?"

I can hear chomping sounds in my ear, the mastication of some malevolent beast. Fear spikes pain in the base of my brain.

"You fucking bastard!" I shout. Pounding heartbeats ring in my ears.

"Who? Me?" says Darrel, disappearing even further into the cover of the frame, only fingertips and eyes showing.

"No, not you. That fucking Sam. I saw him taking notes or some shit. He told them I was high." I spring out of bed, energised by outrage, ready to fight anyone and everyone.

"What? It wasn't Sam," says Mum. "Roger told them."

"Roger, the guy who sweats all the time?"

"He has a thyroid problem."

"He's got a fucking garlic problem."

"Don't start. You're clearly the one who needs help. I'm sorry, Michael, but it's time for some tough love."

"And what does that mean?"

"Sam tried to cover for you, but Roger said you were definitely high. Of course they asked me, and as a mum, my first instinct was to protect you. But how are you going to learn that way?"

I bunch my fists, take a step towards her. "What did you do?" I say. My voice is hoarse from a dry throat.

"I've only recently got off the factory floor myself," she pleads, backing away, hands up in supplication. "You know what it means to me to get the promotion into the office. The managers stood there looking at me and looking at me, and well, I cracked."

"You sold me out."

"Roger was the one who told on you. All I said is you were acting weird. And well, you disappeared and all without telling anyone."

"I told Sam."

"Sam doesn't have any authority."

I think of him putting his arm around my shoulder, guiding me this way and that, telling me what to do—it seemed like he knew what he was talking about at the time. I feel lied to, but it's too easy to blame him. What has he really done? I shake my head, regretting the drugs and their effect on me, a first tinge of remorse penetrating my anger.

"It's for the best," says Mum. "You can't go on like this."

"So you're kicking me out as well? I lose my job, and now this shit?"

"You're not staying here if you're smoking."

"Darrel says you smoke too."

"Thanks again for that, Daz," says Mum dryly. Darrel retreats fully, his fingers and eyes snapping back off the doorframe and disappearing.

I want to put up more of a fight, argue more and defend my position, but I see a vision of me with my fists bunched, Mum with her hands up, afraid of me, and realise it's what has just happened. I feel ashamed. I'm a grown man now—I'm not living up to what I could be. Instead, I see an echo of my dad in myself. Memories flood back, reliving all the moments of terror as a child, watching him threaten and beat my Mum. Dad was bad enough. Now she's stuck with losers like Darrel...

And losers like me.

My shoulders slump in resignation, my fists unclenching. I glance at the weed on the table.

"I'll pack my stuff and go," I say, raising my hands to Mum, not in anger, not to hurt, but in forgiveness, wrapping her up in a hug. She cries in my arms and I kiss her forehead.

***

The open road stretches out before me. I feel a weight lifted off my shoulders, a burden I didn't know I was carrying. Of course I tried to leave the weed behind, but with no money it's not like I could throw it out, or, worse, leave it for Darrel. So I took it and some clothes, and that's about it. Free and light, or so it seems for now, but in my pocket there is something heavy and dense, like an anchor seeking to drag me back down into the depths.

I shift in my seat and readjust my shorts. My fingers brush the corn cob pipe through the fabric. It feels hot like molten lead. I fish it out, consider throwing it away. Instead, it springs from my hand onto the passenger seat. There it travels alongside me as I push up the east coast, past Brisbane and beyond, taking the highway north through Queensland towards a new life. The wind blows through the window, cooling me down and banishing the thoughts which would otherwise stagnate there and poison me like a toxic cloud.

I glance in the rear-view mirror. I see teeth there, chewing up my past. I know there's no going back. The easy feeling leaves me, and instead I flee in fear from something I can't hide from. There is only running away, and this is what I'm doing, running from my problems. I look at the corn cob pipe.

Running from my problems, or taking them with me wherever I go?

I put my foot down and drive faster.

***

The roads become worse, the scenery more beautiful the further north I go. I rarely stop, barely slow down, blaring music through my phone—jacked into the car's speakers—to keep me pumped and awake. There's missed call notifications on the screen. I ignore them. I don't want to talk to Mum anymore.

I'm smoking too much, too quickly. The reassuring words of Black Sabbath's *Sweet Leaf* on repeat convinces me I'm alright, but I know the situation is growing dire as my bag of weed dwindles to stems and crumbs. Rummaging around with pinching fingertips, one eye on the bag, the other on the road, I load the pipe. It is a greedy, hungry maw, open wide to take all I can feed it. Loaded up, the pipe is placed between my pinched lips and I make fiery sacrifice at an altar to a god I do not understand. I don't want to know them, or anyone. In fact, I want to forget, and the drug does its job as it ignites in the pipe, a burning ember taking away the thoughts which crowd in on me from all around. But it is just a blanket I wrap around my head, muffling the sound rather than banishing it. The muted noises turn into new voices as I hallucinate, no longer relaxed by the drug, only wired, not daring to sleep and waste what little high time I have left.

I know soon I won't have this support, the crutch yanked away. I have no money for more weed, and no connections so far up the coast anyway. In a choice between drugs, food, and fuel, fuel has to be the winner as it's the real thing driving me forward, away from my problems and towards a hope of a better future. Luckily the weed is suppressing my appetite, but when it's gone the hunger pangs will return and I don't know what will happen then. I press my foot down harder, the road blurring into a grey snake. I chase after its head as it hisses sweet promises in my ear—I can lie down and rest if only I can catch it.

Worse than the weed situation is the tobacco, and while I still have a decent amount, I know the withdrawals from *that* will be hell and make the lack of weed unbearable. My only chance is to get to my destination as quickly as possible, get myself on a boat and make some money. I look at the fuel gauge. The orange light next to it is on. I don't have much left in me.

Frantic to deny reality, my fingers claw desperately for more—they pinch nothing but air in the empty bag. The weed is all gone, the pipe having swallowed it whole. I tug it from my mouth and stare at its hole in disbelieving accusation.

"You've taken everything," I say. "There's nothing left."

At the same moment, the car sputters and curses me as it conks out. I drift it to the side of the road, still hundreds of kilometres from my destination, and there it lies dead. I'm not much better, destitute and broke. I was hoping to live in the car while I searched for a job on a boat, now I can't even sell the damn thing.

I get out, look left and right on the desolate stretch of highway. Beyond a line of scrubby bush on the far side of the road, the ocean roars and rumbles—it is hungry, and it wants more than I can give it. But as I stand there, the last effects of the drug fading, I realise it is not the ocean but my stomach which is rumbling and growling. I have no way of feeding it either, nothing to give it except my own flesh. The ocean keeps calling though, as if it would be satisfied if I fed it my body.

I load the pipe with a small portion of tobacco, trying to ration out what remains to keep the withdrawals at bay as the weed wears off. It barely scratches the surface of the cravings. I stand on the side of the road, my thumb up in the air, accompanied in parallel by the jaunty angle of the pipe in my mouth. It's like we're in this together, but I don't want this partner anymore, even though, when a car finally does stop for me, I feel it's stopping more for the pipe than I—through morbid curiosity or some bizarre spell, I don't know. I climb into the back of a truck.

"No smoking back there," says the driver. The gas cylinders clink around me, seeking to crush me with their metal weight full of lighter than air gas. It's ironic.

I hunker down, not wanting to be here but having no choice. It feels like all ability to make choices left me a long time ago, and I don't know why. Even coming north feels forced now, not of my free will, only inevitable, something calling my name, seeking a piece of me.

I munch on the stem of the pipe, ravenous for any tiny taste of weed or tobacco it can give me. There is nothing but dead fumes, like those rising from a corpse, half obscured by the reek of gas. I have nothing to shield me, and by the time the truck pulls into town, many hours later, I am red raw with the abrasive touch of reality, half mad from the fumes. The driver pauses by a bus stop and I get out. I thank him, the noxious gas pouring from my mouth, my eyes red, and he nods as if he were just doing his duty, playing his part in some larger drama. He goes without me ever learning his name or even looking squarely at his face. He drifts away like a cloud and is gone.

"Can I bum a smoke?" asks a dark skinned man sitting at the bus stop.

I shake my head. "I was going to ask you the same question," I say, pocketing the pipe. It snuggles against the precious dregs of my remaining loose tobacco.

"Oh, in that case," says the man, pulling out a pack. He offers me a pre-rolled cigarette. I take it, thinking of the poor fucker who had to make these in a factory somewhere. It reminds me too much of home but at least the nicotine will take the edge off from the long drive.

"Got any weed?" I ask the man when I've burned down the cigarette in three long drags. My body sings, tingling with relief.

"Got any money?" he says.

"No."

"Then no."

"I'm here to work the fishing boats."

"Good luck to you."

"You think they're hiring?"

"Ain't no one hiring me, brother."

"Oh."

"Yeah, welcome to Cairns."

"Uh, thanks."

***

I sleep rough that night in some bushes by the ocean. Luckily it's warm here. In fact it's just plain hot and there are too many insects. They pester and sting me so I get little rest. In the morning I drink some water from a tap in the park and give myself a bit of a birdbath. There's a lot of people doing morning exercise, working out on the gym equipment and running along the ocean path. Trendy cafes serve people right by the water. I can't even afford a coffee. All I've got is a little backpack with some spare clothes, but that's about it. I smoke a pipe of tobacco to keep the hunger pains down, look thoughtfully out at Trinity Inlet and the ocean beyond. Really though, there's not a lot of thoughts in my head, which I'm grateful for—without the weed mixed in the pipe is blissfully silent, nothing but an old pipe for a change. Even the ocean here is calm, the inlet flat. Further out many boats are already heading off for tourist trips and fishing. My future self goes with them, trailing along in their white wakes to my destiny at sea.

It's getting even hotter as the sun rises, the humidity closing in so that being on land feels claustrophobic and restricted. The air feels thick like molasses, my movements sluggish, my strength sapped by the heat and lack of food. I consider going for a swim, submerge myself in the water and rinse off the feeling of constraint. There, floating freely in the warm water, I could be at peace, the sea enveloping me like the embryonic fluid of the womb. I long for a hug, so I close my eyes, imagine the salt water filling my ears as my head goes under. For a few blissful moments it is like being in a sensory deprivation tank, with no voice screaming at me from the inside or the outside.

Then the seagulls squawk, and someone is rattling around in a bin nearby, loudly fishing for cans. It pulls me back. I get up, more keen than ever to get in the water. I see no one else swimming, and I think they must be mad here, with this heat, to not take advantage of the calm inlet. I take off my shirt and step towards the thin beach beyond the boardwalk. But there is a sign—*Marine stingers may be present in these waters. Crocodiles may be present in these waters*—and this stops me dead. The sign shows a huge jellyfish with long tentacles like those of a mythological sea monster. I imagine these ethereal tendrils wrapping me up, stinging me to death, and I grimace with ghost pains rippling across my skin.

Even worse is the crocodile, with its huge, gaping jaws. It's easy to picture them snapping down powerfully to break rib cages, slicing flesh with its rows of dagger-like teeth. I shudder, glance out at the ocean, which doesn't look so inviting anymore, an ominous air hanging over it like a heat haze, shimmering so as to obscure the future and all the dangers which lurk there.

***

I walk the streets aimlessly, trying to form a plan but not able to, my thoughts muddled with lack of food. Anxiety grips my heart, forcing each beat of blood out painfully through a clenched fist. My skin burns and my tongue turns into dry grit. Stars dance in front of my eyes. In my gut is a dropped rock, splashing into wetness, no substance found there to stop the nausea. The sweat pouring off me is due to much more than just the confusing heat which cooks my brain. The withdrawals from the weed are doing a number on me. Throwing tobacco down this hole does nothing but make me edgier. I suspect the corn cob pipe is toying with me, mocking me, even though its voice is silent—I don't seem to have the energy for hallucinations.

I float aimlessly like a ghost past the bars and restaurants, both open early, with people eating and drinking, laughing and relaxing. I am unseen, unspoken of, a wide-eyed backpacker, perhaps, a faceless nobody who has drifted into town looking for work. I suppose they are right. They ignore me as they play in paradise, carefree. I want to steal their hot chips, the smell of them making my stomach growl. I loiter by a few tables to this purpose, swoop in when people abandon their meals. Each time a waiter or waitress shoos me away like a seagull.

"You hungry, mate?" asks a woman. She's older than some of the other waitresses, most of them young and pretty foreigners. She speaks with an Aussie accent. I put on my best smile and shake my head, not wanting to look pathetic. I hide the handful of chips I've grabbed behind my back, gravy dripping down my leg.

"Look, you can drop that rubbish. Come on in and wash dishes for a half hour and I'll give you a meal," she says, turning and sauntering into the restaurant from which she emerged. She doesn't look back, sure I'm following. My eyes dance along the curves of her figure, which has a come-hither quality.

What really catches my attention, though, is the smell from the kitchen. It grips me by the scruff of my neck and drags me inside with an urgency I've never felt before. The aroma of fresh, hot food gives me a last burst of power, as if the smell itself has weight and substance which fuels me, carries me through the dishwashing when I thought I had no more energy. It even makes me forget the drug withdrawals, which, to be sure, are only phantoms anyway. My mind has gotten ahead of itself, with a lack of access to the drug projecting a future suffering upon me now more than what should be happening to me physically this early. It's all in the mind.

Or the gut—the hot meal of bangers and mash, veggies and gravy goes down with relish, filling up the empty hole in me, making everything seem alright. The world sparkles again. I can actually see the sun, the beach, the sky... the ocean. A wave of dread washes up on my shore. A meal might be something, but it's only one meal. I have nothing else.

The waitress comes up to me, rubs my shoulder. "That hit the spot?" she asks. I can hear some of the care and maternal feeling in her voice. I recoil from it, as her touch says there's more to this than that.

"Thanks, you helped me out of a spot," I say, getting up. "I've got to be going now."

"Wait a second. Come now, I scratch your back..." She lets the words trail off, punctuated with raised eyebrows.

"I already washed the dishes."

"Yeah, I bet you scrub up real nice." Her fingertip trails down my arm, drops off the end of my hand and leads my eyes down with it to a space between her legs. I feel a void inside me opening up again, a desire I can't fulfil, a solution here suggested, but there's more pressing things which can't wait. My lungs ache, a spike of anxiety driving me forward, not knowing the way.

"Look, you're cute and everything. Maybe a bit old for me, though," I say, and wince at her reaction to the last part. She recovers well, though, not letting me off that easy.

"I'm Sharna," she says with an uneven smile and a forced laugh.

"Michael."

"That's a nice name. Why don't you come home with me tonight? I get off at six."

"It's tempting, but no thanks," I say, feeling too coerced, as if caught in a honey trap, unable to pay whatever price will be asked of me next. It seems like this meal was the hook and I'm the catch. I'm prey. She seeks to snap her vagina jaws down upon my head and drag me down into their suffocating embrace.

I get up, chasing my own needs as I'm escaping hers. I walk towards the door, feeling sure I'm going to escape. The exit is so tantalisingly close, the open air, with an infinite ocean beyond. But what happens next stops me dead.

"I've got weed," she says, knowing the right bait.

***

Like a fish caught on a long line, I travel in a loop further into town, thinking I've gotten away. Really I'm tiring slowly, kept on the hook, ready to be reeled back in when I'm spent. For now, though, I find I have some new energy with food in my belly. I smoke my pipe in a jolly fashion, chomping at it as if it were a cigar, occasionally plucking it from my mouth to inspect some shop or other. These seem to repeat in collectives of threes—opal store, dive school, and souvenir stand— over and over, punctuated with the occasional ice cream shop for a bit of variety.

On the corner is a McDonald's, a monolithic monument to Western civilisation, people buzzing in and out of it like flies around a corpse. I steer clear of it, head over towards a splash of turquoise light. Getting closer, I see it's a big pool, open to the public, merging seamlessly with the park and street. It shines like a sparkling jewel, promising relief from the heat. I shed my outer skin—my clothes already damp and smelly with sweat—and wade into the water in my jocks. I feel free, the water clear. It's shallow, easy to see the bottom—nothing lurking there, nothing to fear.

Mere metres away is the ocean, so murky and dangerous, with little ominous waves slapping the boardwalk that separates it from the pool, reminding me the barrier between worlds is thinner than I think. Risk is never far away and change is always looming. Yet I still can't wait to make that jump into the unknown, take on whatever is out there. I need that danger to be free of another, more pressing existential threat. A shiver runs across my body—an anxiety pang brought on from the need for drugs—and I can't wait to untangle the long line hooked into my mouth. I feel it pulling at me, this time through my groin, the other end leading back towards Sharna and our appointment at six.

For now I can forget about that, or at least try to, floating on my back, letting the water rush into my ears and drown out my thoughts. The sun kisses the skin of my face and belly, marking me with its pink blessings. After a while I roll over for it to do the same to my back. I open my eyes and let the chlorinated water sting them a bit. It reminds me of those jellyfish living in the ocean, waiting to wrap me up, and suddenly the sun's rays feel like a lash on my back. I stand up with a start, the water cascading off me as if I'm sloughing off a membranous layer, scourged free of my flesh by the sun. My skin tingles all over, and I recognise it as drug withdrawals, only partially muted in their intensity by the cool touch of the water as I submerge myself, trying to escape.

Under the water I see swimming bodies. They're lithe and fluid, with the grace of hunters closing in. I burst from the water in time to see dorsal fins closing in on me. My blood runs cold, but the fin is flesh coloured, human. It's some kids pretending to be sharks with praying hands. It's all pretend, made up in my head, or in the head of someone else. Even so, I flinch again, feeling the harsh lash of the sun on my raw skin. Turning, I see a giant jellyfish in the sky, sun ray tentacles reaching for me. It's nothing but a cloud, yet I flee from it all the same, wading from the water, my panic a personal affair, not infectious, not spreading to the holiday makers all around. They go on with their blissful lives, their problems opaque to me, my own seeming transparent and obvious, yet ignored.

Do they have no sympathy? I'm hurting, I think.

Thoughts of Sharna and the escape route open to me return, even though I know it's not the escape I want, just the easy way out. I fight against it, feeling the tug of the line now, the hook buried deep in my mouth. It prevents me from speaking up against myself, questioning my motives. In a blind attempt at getting free, I pull and fight. Gathering up my clothes, I put them on and walk. My struggles take me further along the shore, trying to put some distance between me and the restaurant, knowing always that the hook is still there, the line just played out further, and that I can't outrun this thing.

I take out a fresh set of clothes and change into them, trying to at least look respectable. The same can be said of a big building I pass, glammed up like a pig wearing makeup. I recognise the Mandarin characters for 'casino' on the sign—some vestige of a high school class, now mostly forgotten—even as the English words by its side, which should be much clearer, blur into meaningless. There is gravity to the building, despite its faded glory, and I would feel the pull of this addictive allure—with all its promise of solving at least one of my problems—if I didn't have much more pressing concerns. I look at my phone, see there's still plenty of time before six, and this makes me both sick and happy. There's space to move, space to breathe, and I deceive myself into believing I can use it. I see something up ahead which gives me hope of getting away.

It's the port, lined with boats—my ticket out of here, away from myself.

***

I'm drawn by the smell more than anything. It seems to exist on a sliding scale, from the pristine freshness of a salt breeze up by the luxury yachts, through to a crescendo of fishy stench down by the trawlers. The seagulls help point the way as well, a huge boiling swarm of them, filling the air and jetties with their bodies and piercing cries as they squabble over access to their prize. I have to elbow my way through them, just another scavenger, here to get what scraps I can. I'm treated with much the same contempt by the crews of the fishing boats, who ignore my words. My questions and petitions are nothing but wailing and squawking to their ears. I wave my arms to get their attention, looking all the more like a bird for it, and they laugh, chuck me a titbit, a bloody chunk of fish guts that smacks me in the face and slides down my once clean clothes, now ruined by a smear of red gore.

My ears burning red with humiliation, I turn to retreat along the pier, hounded the whole way by the echoes of the fishermen's laughter and the seagulls pecking at my shirt.

***

There are doors ahead. I nearly run into them in my blind flight, but, thankfully, they open automatically, admitting me passage into another world. The contrast is stark, the burning heat of the day outside replaced with the coolness of air conditioning inside, the glare of the sun shifting to the fluorescent glow of lighting tubes, and the pungent reek of fish guts toned down to a sterile, salty freshness of uncooked seafood. The gladiator's ring of the pier—with its blood and guts and flashing steel knives—has been exchanged with clean rows of prepared fish, lobsters, shrimp, oysters, squid, and more, all neatly arranged on ice, little signs designating the price that must be paid in homage of their deaths. I'm in the fish market.

The shoppers have neat plastic baskets and the men behind the glass cabinets have quaint striped aprons. People are smiling... until they see me. With the fish guts smeared on my face and shirt, I am a gross effigy of a part of their world they would prefer to have kept on the far side of the door, isolated and contained. I've brought the stink in with me. The blood—entirely absent from this shop front fantasy—is now on full display, reminding everyone of their carnivorous and possibly cannibalistic intentions. They look ashamed, or disgusted, and turn away, quickly heading for the checkouts, but not before surreptitiously sliding whatever flesh they crave into their baskets.

I buckle under the weight of their scrutiny. Head down, I run the gauntlet of their judgement. Not willing to go back the way I have come, but wanting to escape, I take the other way out, back into town. This door isn't automatic, and I smack into it painfully. More embarrassment flushes my features. I rub my stinging nose. My hand comes away with blood on it. I can't tell if it's mine or belongs to the fish.

My anxiety building, a panic attack imminent, I rush along the line of restaurants, not knowing what time it is, but hoping the countdown is close to the magical number. I have to run yet another gauntlet—the alfresco dining of the strip means there are people on every side as I push through the crowds. Those seated at the tables tuck in bibs to stop the juices from staining their nice clothes as waiters bring them trays of fresh seafood. The crack of lobster and crab shells, the steaming flesh rising to the nostrils, picked up and crammed into hungry, chewing mouths—it is a grotesque kaleidoscope of sensation shifting around me as I run.

"Feed me or I'll swallow you whole," I hear a voice say. I look around in fear, but all I see are ruddy red faces laughing and eating, shoving the ocean's harvest down into their guts. The voice repeats, becoming more familiar with each echoing cadence, until I recognise it as my own, bouncing around inside my head. I clutch desperately at my chest with one hand, at my pocket with the other. Both my heart and the corn cob pipe throb painfully, straining to take the load of anxiety I have placed on them, one struggling to pump life through me, the other to drain it, promising nothing but a slow death.

***

"You're a bit early, honey," says Sharna as I stumble into the restaurant where she works. I hear her say the word *honey* and it's more evident than ever that I've walked into a trap, the floor sticky like molasses, though that might be from spilled beer. This whole town feels sticky, the heat cloying, my clothes plastered to my skin, revealing what's beneath in a way which makes Sharna eye me up and down with an odd look like she's ready to devour me. I feel like one of those lobsters, cracked open, exposed, the flesh hot and moist. The will to live has been boiled out of me by the heat of this town, my body steamed in muggy humidity.

"You been in a fight or something?" asks Sharna, a flash of excitement in her eyes, a crazy sparkle like the wink of a lunatic full moon. I look down at my stained shirt and sniff the blood caked around my nostrils.

"Guys down the pier," I say.

"You certainly smell like the pier. Go scrub up in back. You know the way." She taps my butt to hurry me along. I feel like cattle herded into a pen, or perhaps a naïve newborn baby slapped by the doctor, alerted to the presence of pain in a wider world, the womb torn away from me. I'm desperate for a return to that safe space, a familiar embrace, so I'm willing to hug this banshee close to get my fix.

I go in back, give a nod of recognition to the kitchen staff as I walk to the sink. They give me knowing looks, sly smiles, as if I'm part of a routine they've seen before. I frown, splash soapy water on my face, scrub at my shirt like I had the dishes hours earlier. It feels like I work here now, and maybe I do, maybe this is how people get a job. If one of the guys at the harbour had been interested in me I'd be working a boat right now rather than hovering over a sink full of dirty dishes. Everyone is looking for their piece of something. I try to think of the weed and ignore the rest, heading back out to the main part of the restaurant.

"You want a drink while you wait?" Sharna asks, and I nod, desperate for relief from myself and from this town.

She places me in the corner like a piece of furniture, installs a beer in front of me, gives me a little tap on the head like I'm a dog she's telling to stay. She goes back to work. I'm left to people watch. The tourists in their gaudy holiday clothes float by like colourful fish in an aquarium, except I'm in the tank with them, and I'm drowning, the beer lifted to my lips and inhaled instead of air.

***

I don't drink often, so the single beer has a bit of an effect on me, taking off the edge of my paranoid anxiety and leaving my mind drifting aimlessly. Unfortunately, I don't have money for more, and I'm too proud to ask Sharna for another.

Not too proud for a drug hand out, though, I think, but add darkly, *Yeah, but I'm going to have to pay for that one way or another.*

She'll have her pound of flesh, that's for sure. I watch her glide past, sleek and smooth like a shark, deadly and mysterious. She's twice my age, but I like that, feel like I'm getting a real woman, someone who should be out of my league. It's hard to explain, but there's a sense of a bargain, of value gained, like I must be worth something for her to bother circling around me, eying me out the side of one eye. But that's what a shark would do.

She's not so bad looking, really—just plain, forgettable if I got a glimpse of her on the street. I like her hair though. It's blonde, with part of it dyed black up on the underside of her ponytail. It's what I would call bogan chic, complementing the faux diamond stud masquerading as a beauty spot above her lip. Her chandelier style belly button piercing hangs down her exposed midriff, completing the aesthetic.

I can't judge. I'm not much more of a catch, though I have the sparkle of youth she seems to be drawn to. She carries past a plate of crocodile pies, another of kangaroo sausages, and she winks at me like I'm next, but whether I'm to be served as a customer or a meal is not clear. She smiles. Her teeth are too small, too sharp for her to ever be truly pretty. I smile back, glancing at my phone, and realise it's finally approaching the appointed hour. A part of me wants to run away, but not the greater part, which desperately needs the drugs to feel normal. I was kind of hoping to leave that all behind me, go through the withdrawals on the trip up the coast, and be over it by the time I got here. I should have known my problems would follow me. They aren't caused by the factory, or Mum, or Darrel, or any of it, after all. They are inside me, a part of me, something I carry with me. I don't want to still be carrying them when I get on a boat, so I make a promise this is the last hurrah, a final fling.

Sharna comes over and tosses her apron down on the table in front of me as if she's sloughed off a second skin. She faces me head on, both her eyes fixed on me, the shark turned at bay, ready to close in for the final kill. I gulp down a lump in my throat, and I feel similarly swallowed myself as she devours me with her eyes. She scoops me up out of my seat with a jerk of her head, which I obey like a dumb puppet with its strings yanked. There is a tug somewhere else as she grabs my hand and plants it on her butt. She waves goodbye to her co-workers, who shake their heads knowingly, or give me a look of pity. Confused and torn between desires, not knowing which to feed and which to starve, I let Sharna make choices for me which I should make myself. She leads me to her car and gets behind the wheel, takes me wherever it is she's taking me.

***

She's kissing me hungrily as we burst through the door of her apartment, cutting my lips with her sharp little teeth. I taste blood, and I assume so does Sharna, as it seems to drive her into an even greater frenzy of ravenous lust. Her body feels all angles and bones, no softness as she grinds into me, tenderising my flesh. Even her lips feel sharp to me, nipping at the skin of my neck like a piranha's. I try to push her off me, to gain some space, but she's latched on, a parasite, a lamprey hanging as limp as my dick. She touches it.

"What's the matter? Don't you like me?" she asks.

I don't answer.

"I like you," she says, as if that's all that matters here. She unzips my jeans. I zip them back up.

"Could we have a smoke first?" I ask, turning my back on her and walking further into her gloomy apartment. The place has a musty unlived in smell. Moonbeams cast spectral shadows on the walls. I see Sharna's dark silhouette looming over me, hands outstretched, reaching for me with elongated fingertips. I spin on the spot, try to catch her out, but she's now on the opposite side of me, switching on a lamp. It banishes the blue glow of the moon, replaces it with a soft yellow light which seems more human. In its illumination I see Sharna's face, flushed with lust and frustration. She sits on a mouldy couch, pokes her pointy fingers around in a bowl on the table like a witch scrying the future in a fish's entrails. I see my fortune in those chopped green leaves and ground up buds. The corn cob pipe springs from my pocket as if it were conjured by a magic trick. I sit myself down, already reaching for the bowl.

"What the hell is that?" asks Sharna.

"What?" I say, my fingers dipped into the green.

"Is that a fucking corn cob pipe?"

"Yeah, so?"

"It looks pretty gross."

"It belonged to my great-grandfather."

"Okay, that's way gross."

"Got any other suggestions?"

"Maybe use a bong like a normal person."

"Okay, you got one?"

"Yeah, under the table."

I reach down and pull out the inevitable homemade job.

"Gatorade bottle, classic," I say, giving it a spin. "Watermelon chill flavour."

"Got to get your electrolytes somehow," says Sharna with a manic laugh.

I frown as I check the Blu Tack seal around the garden hose stem. "At least you've got a copper cone piece. I was expecting foil."

"They sell them at the markets if you know which stalls to ask at."

"It'll do the job," I say, the verdict of a connoisseur. Sharna sniggers as I load up a cone. "Sorry, you want first?" I ask her.

She hands me a lighter. "No, you go ahead, honey. You need it more."

I take a long breath in and out, my body preparing itself for the change that is soon to wash over it. Putting my lips against the mouthpiece, it tastes like Sharna, and cuts me just as much, but I ignore this, apply suction as the flame touches the packed cone. It crumbles, transforms into bright embers, disintegrating to become smoke pulled through the body of the bong, obscuring the insides. The bubbles chug through the fouled water, the pressure building until it is almost unbearable. My thumb releases the shot hole, a finger for a trigger, firing the drug up out of the bong and into my lungs. It smacks up into my brain, down into my guts. The tension peaks inside of me and then dissipates as I breathe out, turning me to mush. The smoke fills my vision and hangs there like a mirage. I look over at Sharna. Through the drug haze, she starts to look good. The sense of danger leaves me even as I realise it was serving a purpose, protecting me through primordial, subconscious instincts. Now those guards are down and I fold under the slightest pressure as Sharna opens her mouth wide. I see those rows of sharp teeth coming for me, but I do nothing to get out of the way, let the drug do the heavy lifting, carrying away all sense of care or self-preservation.

***

The sex is an angry hate fuck. I feel like I'm stabbing her to death with my dick, gutting her like a fish. There's blood. She shrieks as if she's dying. But each time I stop she digs her claws into me, thrusts me back into the breach like I'm a reluctant soldier trying to retreat from the siege.

If there's any pleasure it's only in the approach of the mind rending, climatic ending—it will soon be over and I can smoke again. The orgasm erupts inside me and flows over into her, passing all my anger and frustration from one person to another like poison. To me it's nothing but a release of the tension I feel inside—though I know it will soon return, never fully banished, always looming in the deep, dark waters of my soul, like a predator longing to be fed. To her, it is yet another small death by a thousand cuts she's inflicted on herself, and I'm the latest in a series of blades she wields, using me to scourge her pain with yet more pain which she mistakes for pleasure.

I pull my bloody dick out of her like she's a murder victim—or perhaps this is suicide. She lies still on the floor, face pale and clammy, and my fear returns that I've hurt her, but she's not dead, not physically anyway, though I can't say the same for what lies inside of her. I doubt I could ever bring that part back to life, or even satiate it for a time.

With an effort of the dead resurrected, she sits up, watches my dick deflate, and sighs like I've let her down like all the others. Exposed, covered in her, I feel like a sacrifice tied to a totem pole, smeared in the blood of the victims which have come before me. She gets up, eyes me up and down, deciding if I'm good for much else. A shrug, she passes me on her way to the bathroom. Turning on the hot water, she gets in the shower. I follow, look at her in the mirror, look at myself, her face blue, mine red, the ocean of emotion and the blood of violence reflected back at me, and I wonder if all this is real or just the drugs showing me some hidden layer of existence.

"Can I get in the shower with you?" I ask, desperate to wash the blood off, but just as much to pump some life back into the situation, hold her cool corpse as it warms in the water of the shower. I need to feel human again, actually connected rather than held at a distance, the glass door of the shower between us.

"No," she says, and turns her back on me, the water cascading down her glossy flanks like a fish pulled fresh from the ocean—one I know I have to throw back.

***

Even after my own shower, I feel sticky and ashamed. Post-sex cones only make me feel more confused than comforted, distorting any pleasure into paranoia, the unknown shadows of consequences looming. I sit in shorts on the mouldy couch. The eye of the corn cob pipe watches me from the coffee table, judging me. Sharna comes back from the kitchen, still naked, hands me a bottle of beer like nothing has happened. She cracks the top off her own, the hiss like that of a vicious viper. It makes me jump.

"Edgy," teases Sharna. Her weight dropping down on the couch throws off my equilibrium further. I crack my own beer without looking at it, or her, easing the twist cap off, expecting something to spring out and bite me.

"What's the deal with that pipe anyway?" she asks, half her beer disappearing in three long pulls. I sip at my own, already wasted from the weed and needing little else.

"I told you, it was my great-grandfather's," I say, putting the beer down and picking up the pipe.

"Yeah, but why do *you* have it?"

"I found it. Or it found me, I don't know."

"Creepy."

"My family has a story about it, about how a giant shark ate my great-grandfather."

"Grisly. Wouldn't be the first person a shark took, though, not around here."

"It happened off the coast of the Northern Territory."

"And what, this is his last remaining heirloom, left behind and grieved over by your great-grandmother or some shit?"

"I suppose. Can hardly be the same pipe he was smoking when the shark got him."

"Not unless they caught the thing and cut it open, found it inside him," said Sharna, her face twisting in disgust. "Have you really been smoking out of that thing?"

"Yeah." I twist the pipe in my fingers, frowning. "And no, they didn't catch the shark. We don't even know if it still exists."

"The shark?"

"Do you know what a megalodon is?"

"No."

"It's a species of massive prehistoric shark. They're supposed to be extinct, though some people claim they've seen them."

"Like your great-grandfather, right before it ate him."

"He didn't survive to tell anyone."

"The rest of the crew?"

I shake my head. "Eaten as well."

"Some type of recording?"

"It was back in the fifties."

"Then how the hell do *you* know anything about it? How the hell does anyone know anything about it?"

I pack some weed into the corn cob pipe. "It could all be a hallucination."

"Sounds like one of those stories people tell to make their family sound interesting," says Sharna.

I light the pipe, pull in the smoke. It tastes different than through the bong, the woodiness invoking the distant past once more as if it were yesterday. I see the rows of razor sharp teeth disembowelling human bodies as the jaws of the megalodon crunch down. With a pitiful shriek of fear and phantom pain I throw the pipe down on the coffee table. It clatters like a death rattle.

"What's gotten into you?" asks Sharna, leaning away from me, face contorted.

I point a shaking finger at the pipe. "Give it a try, you'll see."

"I'm not putting something that gross in my mouth."

"Wouldn't be the first time," I mutter.

"What was that, smart arse?"

"You wanted to know how I know. That's how I know."

"You're just tripping, you idiot. Maybe take it easy for a bit. Actually, it's time you were going." She gets up, putting her clothes on to punctuate the point. A wave of panic flushes hot across my skin.

"You're kicking me out?" I ask, incredulous. I eye the weed, wondering if I can take some with me. It weighs much more in the balance than needing a place to sleep, and definitely more than trying for round two of the sex.

"Yeah, we're done, mate. You weren't that good, if I'm being honest. And my son will be home soon."

"You have a son?"

"This might surprise you, but you're not my first."

"That doesn't surprise me at all."

"Alright, up you get." She throws my shirt at me. "And take your shitty pipe with you."

"Can I have some weed at least?"

She crosses her arms. "You've had plenty. Alex will want some after his bar shift."

"Who's Alex?"

"He's my son. Got any more fucking questions?"

"Your son is old enough to smoke weed and work in a bar," I say. It's not a question. My face scrunches up with the dawning realisation that I'm playing the part of Darrel in this drama—the piece of shit deadbeat fucking someone's mum. Alex is probably the same age as me, or close to it. "What the fuck?" I say out loud.

"Go home, Michael," says Sharna.

"I don't have a home."

She slaps her palm to her face, leans her elbow into the other hand. "Christ, mate, what do you want from me? I let you fuck me."

"*You* wanted the sex. I wanted drugs."

"Charming." She gives me a little shove out her front door, starts to close it. I put a hand up to hold it open.

"Wait a second. Please, I need your help."

"With what?"

"I need a job."

***

Feeling discarded, yet too stoned to care much, I crawl under the bushes in the park and fall asleep, drifting into a dark abyss where my future morphs into a dream of the past. The events are conjured by some obscure mind, the phantasm images projected onto the inside of my skull for me to watch before it happens, like a memory remembered in reverse, leading towards the inevitable.

3

Gulf of Carpentaria, off the north coast of Australia, 2025

Death sat like a crust on the surface of the sea as the sun sank low and red on the horizon, a knife's slash across the belly of the whole world. A lonely ship sat bobbing in the crystalline wash. On its deck blood flowed, sloshed around like red wine in a connoisseur's glass. Glinting metal in slick rubber hands cut through the guts of the captives, the process mechanical, economically driven. The fish didn't fight back, mouthing silent groping screams as they struggled to breathe among the masses of their fellows, gills flapping uselessly like torn sails in a squall.

Michael and Tom felt nothing for them as they died, scooping out their steaming entrails, tossing the gutted fish carcasses in a plastic tub like they were so much manufactured product.

"So that's how you got this job?" Tom asked Michael, incredulous.

"What? Shit, no," said Michael. "Sharna got me a job at the restaurant she worked at, and that was enough to keep me alive for a bit."

"I'm surprised she kept you around after she was done with you."

"Trust me, she wasn't done with me."

Tom laughed. "You mustn't have been that bad after all."

"She gave me plenty of practice, don't worry about that."

"Nothing but a vagina monster by the sounds of things."

"I think the term you're looking for is 'man-eater.'"

"Out here that means a totally different thing. You should know, what with that bullshit story about your great-grandfather," said Tom, hefting up the bucket of fish guts and tossing it over the side. Sharks swarmed in the water, snapping up the guts, fighting over them like so many seagulls tossed some chips in the park.

"They certainly lose a bit of their threatening mystique, being around them all the time like this," said Michael, resting a rubber-gloved hand on the railing, watching the sharks thrash around.

"You should still treat them with respect," said Tom, lowering his hand down close to the water, waving it around like so much meaty bait. He pulled it back just in time as a shark jumped up, its jaws snapping shut like a trap in the air where the hand had been a split second before. Tom laughed maniacally as the sharks circled. Their fins shook like raised fists of defiant indignation, cursing their enemies, out of reach in the boat.

"Oh, yes, very respectful," deadpanned Michael.

"They're fucking deadly, I'll give you that much. But a megalodon? No way, the old man would have seen it. He's been coming out this way, what, twenty years?"

"Twenty-three years," growled a voice from beyond the doors of the cabin, sounding like a long dormant volcano finally stirring, rumbling into life. A head emerged, sporting a fiery red beard like an eruption of brilliant lava. "Twenty-three years of dealing with good for nothing scum like you two," said Captain Calvin. "Now get back to bloody work. We're not getting paid by the hour." His head disappeared again like a mole down a hole.

"Bloody work indeed," said Michael, his rubber coveralls slick with gore.

"Don't think we're any better than the sharks, mate. Humans, we're nothing but predators," said Tom, jamming his gutting knife into another fish with self-loathing hate and flicking out the entrails with a well-practiced swipe.

"I'm more annoyed that this isn't all that different than the factory," said Michael, once again doing the same repetitive action he'd been doing all day.

"At least here you get decent pay. And the air is fresh." Tom inhaled noisily and exhaled with a sigh. "Or, at least you eventually get used to it. And hey, it's probably less fishy than that Sharna creature."

Michael snorted, as if trying to clear the stink from his nostrils.

"So," continued Tom, "if she didn't get you this job, how'd you get on a boat?"

"Working in the restaurant, you're around a lot of backpackers," said Michael.

"Fucking bunch of locusts, swarming all over the place," interrupted Tom.

"Okay, boomer."

"Boomer? I'm only five years older than you."

"No boomer bashing," piped in Calvin from the cabin.

Michael rolled his eyes, continued with his story. "I'd drink with the backpackers after work. They bounce around jobs a lot. One of them put me in touch with an agency that gets backpackers temp work, casual positions and such, sometimes seasonal work on the boats. A bit of fancy talking and creative paperwork, and here I am."

"In other words, he conned me and now I'm stuck with his useless arse hundreds of kilometres from home with no one else to gut the fish," said Calvin gruffly.

"You could get Pricey, Jords, or Little T to do it," Michael countered smoothly.

"They're working the nets. You two bozos don't know shit about fish or fishing. I'm not putting you on nets."

"And how will we learn if not by doing?"

"Fucking osmosis for all I give a shit. For now, you do your time with the blood and guts."

"You're never finished with the blood and guts," said Little T with a wink, swinging around a fresh load of fish in a net. It bulged and swelled like a malignant tumour. He pulled a rope and the whole lot dumped at Tom and Michael's feet, a great mound of gulping, drowning creatures, waiting for the sharp metal teeth in Tom and Michael's hands to end their misery with a flick and a twist.

"In a roundabout way, Sharna got you where you wanted to be," said Tom, getting back to work, the movements automatic. "Though, it beats me why you'd so desperately want to be here."

"You're here," countered Michael.

"I have to be."

"No, you don't."

"All this," said Tom sardonically, spreading his arms wide, "will one day be mine."

"It's my boat!" yelled Calvin from the wooden cabin, as if it was his coffin and he was calling out from beyond the grave to deny Tom his inheritance.

"Yes, I know, Dad," said Tom, deflating.

"My dad didn't leave me shit except an emotionally needy mum with a Dad-shaped hole in her heart she filled with a series of deadbeats."

"Sounds like you turned into quite the deadbeat yourself," said Tom with relish, glad to be back talking about the juicy stuff. "Did you ever meet Sharna's son?"

"Yeah, as a matter of fact, I did. He's a good kid."

"Kid? Wasn't he a year older than you?"

"It felt like he was a kid."

"Yeah, because you were banging his mum!"

Michael flushed the colour of the blood sloshing around the deck. "Look," he said defensively, "I'm not a deadbeat."

"Don't stress yourself," said Jords, emerging as if from a shadow. "We've all been there, traded sex for drugs."

"No drugs on the boat!" boomed the disembodied voice of Calvin.

"I'm clean and sober," said Michael proudly.

"You're fucking filthy," said Pricey, a lean giant of a man. He passed with a pat on Michael's back, a bit too hard. "And no one ever said you needed to be sober to work on a boat." He disappeared down into the cabin. There was a clink of glass and soon he and Calvin began to sing very badly.

"I tell you what, I wouldn't mind a bit of weed to deal with that pair of hooligans," said Tom, nodding at the cabin and then looking down at the pile of fish in despair.

"I don't have any, if that's what you're asking," said Michael.

"Sounds like you're really into it though, the stories you tell."

"Yeah, I am. Or was, I don't know. It got its hooks in me, and I knew I wasn't getting away from Sharna if I didn't put my foot down. I kept telling myself I wouldn't go around there anymore. Sure enough, after work, with some drinks under my belt, I'd be round her place, begging for a cone or two."

"Then you'd fuck her guts out, am I right?" said Jords, breathing heavily as he hauled on the ropes. Michael grimaced.

"Yeah, you did," said Tom. He pantomimed the action with his knife and a fish.

"Eventually," said Michael, "I couldn't look at myself in the mirror. So I made the hard choice and gave it up."

"You still got that nasty sounding pipe?" asked Little T, pulling out some rollies and baccy. He rolled himself a smoke with a twist and a lick.

"No, I threw it in the ocean. I've got no use for it anymore."

"Yet you still dredge up that nonsense story about your great-grandfather every other day," said Tom.

"I like it," said Little T. "I love a good shark story." He struck a match, lit his cigarette with it, and threw it over the side as if feeding the sharks a titbit. They ignored it and he scrunched up his face in disappointment. Then one bashed its nose against the hull of the boat, making him jump. He beamed a smile, his whole body shivering with delicious horror. "Fuck, they're terrifying things. To think, all that's between us and them is this flimsy bloody boat. I'm not surprised your great-grandfather copped it."

"You don't believe him, do you?" asked Tom.

"Ever heard of suspension of disbelief?"

"You mean, being gullible as fuck?"

"Alright, that's the last of it," said Jords, straining to bring the final load of fish to hover over the existing pile. With the flourish of a magician, he whipped the net open and a seemingly endless cascade of fish flopped down the sides of the already gigantic mound. Jords tittered darkly. "You boys enjoy gutting those. I think it's time for a drink." He headed for the cabin's hatch. Little T sucked down the last of his cigarette, tossed the butt into the ocean, but didn't look back again as he followed Jords down below, obviously willing to forget the sharks for now.

"But it's getting dark," whinged Tom.

"My bad," said Little T over his shoulder, flicking the switch for the floodlights.

Tom and Michael squinted in the glare of the brilliant beams of white light illuminating the massive pile of fish.

"Let's get to it," said Michael, trying to forget that he now wanted a smoke very badly indeed.

***

The night wore on, grinding numbness overcoming Tom and Michael. Their hands ached from the wet and cold, rubbed raw even through the gloves by the repetitive pressure of the knives cutting flesh. The tubs of gutted fish slowly filled, the mound dwindling bit by bit. Like soldiers set the task of peeling potatoes, the job never seemed to end, and both Michael and Tom felt they were being punished for nothing more than their youth. Additionally, Michael felt persecuted for his naivety. Why did he ever think things would be so much different out here on the sea?

The freedom he sought was an illusion. He could travel no further than a few metres in any direction, hauling the buckets of guts to the railing and tipping them over into a shark infested sea. This boat was a tiny besieged fortress in a sea of rampaging foes, hungry for their blood. One step outside the walls and the crew would be the ones gutted, rather than these poor fish.

We're all prey to something larger and more bloodthirsty, thought Michael, and had to admit that, in the majority of cases, the predator was man himself. The deck was awash with blood he had spilled, all in the name of making money. Rather than freedom, he felt trapped, chained to the need to earn, the irony of it being he needed the money to escape. But where could he go, when even out here in the wide expanses of the sea he felt alone? Tom wasn't much company anymore. Tiredness had done for him, his constant chatter trailing away to muttered murmurs of annoyance at the rest of the crew for leaving them to the backbreaking labour. For a while, the drunken singing of the others had provided some feeling of warmth and humanity to Michael, and he longed to join them in oblivion, but even this promise of release trailed off as the drink pickled everyone into a semi-comatose state.

It didn't help that it was a dark night. The ship's floodlights were turned inwards, a bubble of white to light the deck in a sea of bleak blackness. There was no moon to illuminate the water, and a ceiling of mottled, bruised clouds blotted out the stars. It was like someone had shut him in a box with just a single, flickering candle, and thrown him over the side, so that he was sinking into the depths. Even if he somehow got out of the box, there would be the sharks, waiting to devour him before he could break the surface. He was cut off from the world, cut off from home, with no clear line to the future beside the seemingly impossible completion of this pile of fish. Beyond that, who knew? Probably more fish, a long line of them stretching off into the distance forever, him with a gutting knife in hand, walking that lonely path, with a million fishy souls trailing behind him like ghosts of the slain.

He sighed and dumped a load of guts over the side with a splash like diarrhoea into the shit hole of the world. Michael heard rather than saw the sharks as they went for the stinking mass, their movements sluggish and lazy now. They were probably already full, only eating out of the habit of it, or through fear that tomorrow there would be no more. But there was always more. The ocean was a violent, deadly place. Even the short weeks he'd spent on the boat had taught him that much.

And the only thing keeping me out of the arena of violence is this boat, he thought, then looked back at the scene of carnage on the deck and realised that the line between sea and humanity, between life and death, had blurred to a bloody haze, like a mirage which was doing a poor job of tricking him into thinking he was seeing a vision of a better life ahead. But there was no future. Time had lost all meaning in that long night, so there was only the now—and the now blew chunks.

Jords emerged from the cabin and vomited over the side. The sharks ate even that mess, but they retreated as Jords sprayed them down with the stream of asparagus reeking urine which followed. He taunted them drunkenly, and Michael stared daggers into his back, seriously considered giving him a push over the side, just to show the idiot he wasn't in such an untouchable position as he believed—the liquor couldn't insulate him from life, nothing could. This was a hard lesson for Michael to learn, and it eased his craving for weed a touch, knowing it was his own crutch, actually useless, even as it seemed like a solution to all his problems.

He tore his eyes away from Jords, but saw Tom was giving the man a similar look, one of loathing that was perhaps better directed at his father, who was captain of the ship, and therefore their lord and master. Jords was a symptom. Calvin was the real cause of the ills on board, even if he would never admit it. The captain's age and position was his own insulation from reality, making sure he always had the last word, that he was always right.

There was nothing to be done about it, nothing to alter the pecking order and let Michael and Tom trade places with anyone. Jords sensed their eyes on his back and pitched around, swaying on his feet.

"Fucking sharks," he said to them, leering through squinted eyes, as if he couldn't quite make out who, or what, they were. He reached down, fumbling with his boot, nearly toppling himself over on the slick deck. Wind-milling his arms, there was a flash of brilliance caught in the floodlights. It was like the warning phosphorescence of some poisonous deep sea fish.

"You think you're the next in line?" asked Jords, waving around what Michael realised was a huge Bowie knife. He stabbed the blade in the air, directing his words at Tom. "This isn't your ship, and never will be, alright?"

"I never said it was," said Tom, backing away, the gutting knife in his hand puny compared to the big blade Jords held.

"No? What the fuck are you doing here then? Come to claim your inheritance, haven't you? I've put in ten years with the old man. You think I haven't earned my place?"

"It's just a job, isn't it?" said Michael, instantly regretting it as the Bowie knife turned his way, seeking his heart like the needle of a compass pointing true north. It wavered as if unable to find a settled bearing, navigating more on instinct than an unerring sense of direction.

"You're even worse than him," said Jords, spitting into the muck of guts on the deck. "The last thing we need is some kid off the street that doesn't know shit. You see those sharks out there?"

He jerked his head towards the sea. Michael could hear rather than see the sharks, sloshing about like waves slapping against the hull.

"They think they're the top of the food chain, but they're not," said Jords. "They're nothing but shark fin soup. And that's what the pair of you will be if you get in my fucking way, alright?"

"Okay, mate," said Michael. Tom didn't say anything, but he was shaking all over as if freezing cold.

Jords saw this and laughed. "Maybe I'm giving you too much credit. You're no shark, more a spineless jellyfish."

"Jellyfish can still sting," said Little T, emerging from the cabin. His face glowed orange as he cupped his hands, lit a cigarette. A plume of smoke rose up from his mouth, as if his words had taken on a corporeal form. The smoke drifted over into Jords' face, clouding his vision, a challenge he tried to wave away like an annoying insect, using his knife like a flyswatter.

"Fuck," said Jords, catching his own nose with the swish of the blade. It was just a nick, but it started to bleed profusely. The blood flowed down into Jords' mouth, and when he smiled it was the malevolent red grin of an angry demon, the teeth leering in a shadow face, silhouetted against the backdrop of the floodlights.

"Cut yourself shaving there," said Little T. He leaned casually against the railing, looking out over the shark infested sea as if it were a peaceful view across a summer valley.

"I'll fucking cut you shaving if you fuck with me," Jords spat at him, but Little T chuckled, shook his head.

"There are plenty of monsters out there with bigger teeth than you, cuzzie," he said, not looking back. "Worth remembering the damage they can do if you try to bite them."

Jords made a sound like a caged lion and kicked a fish in impotent rage. He stomped down on another so its guts burst out like a squeezed tube of toothpaste. He raised his Bowie knife as if to plunge it into Little T's back, but instead he spun on the spot, buried it into the wood of the cabin's doorframe with a growl of furious frustration. It sat there quivering like an arrow through the heart of a target.

"The captain won't like that you've wounded his ship," said Little T.

Jords struggled to pull the knife free again, but it was stuck hard. Little T came over, gripped it with his massive ham-like fist, and tugged it clear. Even though Jords was the taller of the two, Little T was the bigger man and seemed to loom large as he calmly handed the knife back.

"Here you go, cuzzie," he said. "Put it away now. Someone might get hurt." The smile on Little T's face was a rictus grin, all the warmth in it frozen over by the ice in his words. With a snarl, Jords snatched back the knife, retreated into the dimly lit cabin. Michael and Tom looked at each other, up to their armpits in gore, with bloody knives in their hands.

"Keep your noses clean," said Little T, flicking his butt over the side and returning to the cabin as well.

***

Dawn burst like a bomb going off in Calvin's skull. He saw stars even before the light of the sun pierced his eyelids and forced them open despite the gunk sealing them shut. He groaned, tried to roll away from the light, but there was no escaping now consciousness had returned to claim him like a Grim Reaper after his soul. The pain was a familiar one. It felt as if the sponge of his brain had been wrung out, and, dry and raw, bounced roughly around on its moorings of tortured nerve cables. Knowing there was no escape, except maybe time or the hair of the dog that bit him, he got up, his stomach lurching like a rough sea even though the boat seemed level and calm. He stumbled uneasily to the cabin door, his skin grey, a hand held to the band of agony across his forehead.

"You blokes still at it?" he said as he emerged onto the deck, squinting against the brilliance, his tongue rough like sandpaper. He wasn't referring to his useless son and the even more useless temp worker he'd accrued like so much flotsam and jetsam washed up on his shores. Nor was he referring to his other, more experienced crew members, still huddled around their bottles, looking and smelling far worse for wear, even by the standards of those who lived and worked on a fishing trawler. No, he was talking to the sharks, who circled his boat like an adoring crowd come to cheer their beneficent benefactor returned. He raised a hand, either to fend off the sunlight or to accept the silent cheers of his predacious kin, it wasn't clear to an observer which.

"We caught a lot of fish. It's a lot of work gutting this many," said Tom wearily in his defence, even though his father wasn't talking to him. The crew didn't even bother to acknowledge or defend their intoxication, well aware the poison in their blood flowed directly from the captain.

Calvin shook his head in annoyance, as if responding to both the words of Tom and lack of them from the others. But really he was trying to clear a bad memory, a vision of Tom's mother, who was even uglier than himself, if truth be told. He looked at his son.

No wonder he's got a face like a dropped pie, the poor bastard, he thought.

"This should be the last tub," said Michael, looking chipper, as if the sun's rays gave him energy which overcame the lack of sleep and hard work he had endured through the night.

The vigour of youth, lamented Calvin, feeling the meagre energy he had remaining in this life draining from his bones like liquor from a bottle. He grunted, not wanting to acknowledge the boy. Instead, he jerked his head at the rest of the crew. "What the fuck are you sitting around for?" he asked. He didn't care that they were drunk, but he did care that the sun was well up and the stacked tubs of fish sat out in the heat. That was money. "Get those tubs down in the hold packed in ice already. And don't give me that insolent look, Jords. I'll ram that fucking Bowie knife right up your arse if you look at me like that again."

Pricey was the first to his feet, extending like a long spring. He'd undoubtedly gotten some sleep otherwise he'd be totally useless now, being nearly as old as Calvin. The other two were slower to rise. There was an edge to Jords and Little T, like long dormant volcanoes smouldering, ready to blow at any minute. The tension was palpable as they stared at each other, their locked gaze seeming to be the only thing which kept them steady as they got to their feet. They both had their hand on a single bottle, and electricity seemed to be jumping between the two of them through this conduit.

Calvin stomped over and grumpily snatched the bottle. The tie cut, the two men fell apart, seemed to forget each other existed, and, with Pricey, began to haul the crates of fish below deck mechanically, their auto-pilots engaged. The captain took a swig of the bottle. It tasted rancid, though it was booze, so it smoothed the jagged edges of his existence a little as it seeped into his sponge brain.

"Can we turn in?" asked Tom. His voice was thin, small like that of a tiny boy begging for relief from an arduous chore.

Calvin turned on him angrily, his thoughts sloshing around like the liquor in the bottle, his hate of Tom's mother projected onto the lad. But the projection struck a mirror, and the hate was self-hate reflected as he realised here was nothing but a smaller version of himself asking for relief. Calvin's insides softened a little, but he remembered his own dad, and the softness he felt froze in his guts like ice. There had been no relief for him in his youth, and it had made him who he was today.

If you count that as a good thing, he thought bitterly to himself.

"This is my boat," he said out loud, as if challenging the inner voice. Tom looked at him questioningly. "So, no," said Calvin. "You can haul the tubs with the others."

He turned his back on all of them, pleased to have done a good day's work, and retreated back to the cabin with the bottle.

***

"Well, this is a bunch of bullshit," said Michael, but Tom was too tired to complain. His muscles ached, his eyes felt dry and sore. Plus, the other crew were working hard as well, so they were in no mood to hear any griping.

Yeah, but they weren't up all night gutting these fish, thought Tom. Michael elbowed him as if trying to rouse him from his sleepwalking slumber, but he had nothing but a grunt to offer in return, the last of his will drained away by the altercation with his father, just the latest in a long string of instances of neglect and abuse ranged across his whole life.

Jords sniggered as if reading his feelings, sucking on them like the emotional leech he was. Little T was too busy working to offer him any form of defence.

"What you laughing at?" said Michael, and Tom looked at him with moist eyes, not even grateful, just close to breaking, knowing another run in with anyone would push him over the edge.

"Michael, don't," croaked Tom.

"I'll fucking lock you in the freezer, you give me any more lip," Jords said to Michael. "It's not like the captain will notice. Not quick enough at any rate."

"No one is going in the freezer," said Little T levelly. "You remember what happened last time?"

"Last time?" said Michael.

A shiver of cold ran through Tom's body at the memory. He shook his head as if trying to warm himself, his teeth chattering in fear.

"If anyone gets on that radio and calls the feds again, I'll gut them myself," said Jords, looking meaningfully at Tom as he passed with a tub in his arms.

"What's he mean by that?" Michael whispered to Tom. Tom shook his head, knowing but not willing to even speak of the code of silence the fishermen adhered to out here while at sea. Even Little T and Pricey nodded sagely at the wisdom and correctness of Jords' statement.

What happens on the boat, stays on the boat, thought Tom. *And only the captain has the power to intervene.*

Tom looked at the cabin door as he walked towards the stairs into the hold with yet another tub.

But he has no desire to save me, even while predators swirl around me.

Tom's eyes swivelled to Jords, and then out at the ocean and the sharks there. A spike of fear rammed up his butt, his cheeks clenched so tight he froze on the spot, ramrod straight. He started to shake so much he dropped the tub of fish, their gutted carcasses spilling at his feet.

"Oi, watch it," said Pricey, elbowing past.

Tom took no notice of him, his eyes fixed out at sea, wide with horror. There was a shadow looming on the horizon. Tom recognised the massive shape of it from Michael's story, even if he didn't believe in the thing he saw with his conscious mind. His subconscious filled in all the details though, spreading fear through his body as his imagination caught up with a reality he was seeing but not wanting to see.

He blinked repeatedly, believing his tired eyes were failing him, and that the object would disappear once focused on. But it got larger and firmer in his sight with each blink, moving from the realm of the imperceptible to the tangible, there to cause havoc with his already shredded nerves. He rubbed his eyes in growing panic, and it was like clearing the lens of a telescope with a cloth. The shape he saw came instantly into focus and was magnified by the swiftly closing distance as it powered forward on fins with the propulsion force of outboard motors. It was cut from the same cookie-cutter silhouette as the sharks around it, but on a much grander scale. The dorsal fin towered out of the water like the sail of a sailing boat, and the mouth opened wide enough for Tom to walk into it, there to disappear forever, swallowed down the gullet of this monster with the rest of its prey.

Tom uttered a single ominous word, not believing he was actually saying it, but knowing the truth of it all the same.

"Megalodon."

***

The word was like a grenade lobbed into the fishing trawler, and the reactions of the men on board were as varied as they themselves were. Not all of them saw or understood the danger even as the seconds to detonation ticked down.

"What's that, cuzzie?" said Little T, perking up with excitement, a boyish glimmer in his eye as he turned to look out upon the sea.

"Can we get back to work?" said Pricey, his back turned to the horrific monster running down on them like a freight train as he hefted another tub.

"Holy shit, it's fucking real!" said Michael, horror and wonder playing across his face in equal measure. He reached for a pipe in his pocket which wasn't there.

Jords squeaked in terror, instinctively pulled the weapon from his boot. Suddenly, the huge Bowie knife looked tiny.

Then the megalodon spoke, its jaws snapping shut with a percussive bang, spraying them all with a shower of gore.

***

The monster wasn't going for the boat. There was more immediate prey to be had in the great shoals of lesser sharks who, in their panic to escape, had bunched together in a confused crowd, boxed in and cut off from escape by the hull of the trawler. The megalodon scooped several of them into its yawning mouth, biting down as it glided past the boat, its tubular bulk like that of a surfaced submarine streaming water from its huge, glossy flanks.

A wash of blood squirted from the munched sharks as they were speared and torn by teeth the length of a man's arm. This was followed a second later by a wave of salt spray as the megalodon completed its attack run and its colossal mass splashed down into the water. The crew of the trawler were first drenched in the red blood and then cleansed with the blue sea, an ocean baptism both bitter to the taste and stinging to the eyes. The twin waves hit them like the backhanded swipe of a displeased god, knocking them from their feet, the megalodon showing its contempt as it disappeared beneath the water again. The crew sloshed and flailed about, spluttering and cursing on a deck awash with water pinked with blood.

"It's fucking real!" repeated Michael, jumping up and nearly going arse over once more as he slid across the deck as if it were slick ice. He bumped against the railing and leaned over to look into the water, but the megalodon was nothing more than a dark shimmering blur, sinking deeper into the sea each second, small now so that it felt like the whole thing had been an illusion, a trick of the eye by a talented magician, able to make things appear and disappear at will.

"Don't get a man all excited there, fella," said Little T, coming up beside him and clasping him on the shoulder. He was quivering all over in fear, yet smacking his lips as if savouring a fine meal. He was consumed with the thrill of delicious terror.

"You saw it, the megalodon?" Michael asked him.

"I didn't see nothing," interrupted Pricey, lumbering over like a lanky giant. He flicked fish guts from his shoulders with a grimace, more annoyed than disgusted.

"The sharks are pissing themselves, scattering every direction," said Jords with a laugh of haughty condescension. "Look at 'em run, the bloody cowards."

"I heard the girly noise you made when the megalodon showed up," said Michael, raising his eyebrows with a sideways glance. "I wouldn't be saying anything, if I were you."

"You calling me a coward?" said Jords, his pitch rising hysterically. He automatically reached for his boot, and, when he found the knife wasn't there, he seemed to remember that he'd been holding it, and now it was gone. His head swivelled in all directions, eyes darting like a cornered rat.

"Not such a big man without your knife, are you?" said Michael. His eyes were shards of ice.

Jords growled like a stirring bear.

"Easy there, tiger, we got bigger fish to fry," said Little T, his hand still clamped hard down on Michael's shoulder, the fingers biting into the skin, knuckles white.

"That was a true to God megalodon. Fuck me, talk about a monster."

"So I'm not losing my mind. It's real?" asked Michael.

"Oh, yes," said Little T breathlessly, fat beads of sweat forming on his forehead.

"I can't tell if you're scared or excited."

"Can't I be both?"

"Easy now throwing around the M-word," said Pricey.

"You afraid to even call it by what it is?" said Michael.

Pricey shook his head sagely, as if he'd seen it all before and was schooling the naivety of youth. "It could have been anything. Probably nothing but a whale messing with the sharks."

"I saw something, cuzzie," said Little T. He let go of Michael, pumped his fists in the air like a child excited on Christmas morning.

"Yeah, that's right," said Pricey. "You saw s*omething*, but not *that*."

"It was a megalodon," said Tom from behind them, his voice small and distant, so creepily eerie that they all turned to look at him.

"Come, lad, how would you know, eh?" said Pricey. "Maybe it *was* a big shark, but if so nothing more than an unusually large great white scaring off its smaller cousins."

"What great white is as long as this boat? What great white could consume several other sharks in one gulp?" Tom's voice was reed thin, his gaze distant and unfocused as if he'd seen a ghost.

"Its dorsal fin did clear the railing here," said Little T, giving the barrier a pat, then snatching his hand away as if it were hot, realising it no longer provided the protection he'd once thought it did.

"And its jaws, mate, fuck me, they opened taller than a man," said Michael, swept up in the moment, channelling the spirit of ancient blood in his veins.

"Alright, alright," said Pricey, "now we're really getting into 'I caught a fish this big' territory."

"We've got to tell the captain."

"Oh, no, no, no." Pricey shook his head vehemently. "I'm not disturbing him for this nonsense."

"But he'll want to go after it, won't he?" said Little T, a mad sparkle in his eyes.

"What? Fuck no."

"You don't know that. He might."

"He hasn't crawled out of a bottle for much of anything in years. What makes you think this wild goose chase will get him to?" said Jords. He found his knife on the deck among the scattered fish, held it aloft in triumph like a trophy.

"No one said anything about stopping drinking," said Little T.

"I gave up all alcohol and drugs. It was the best thing I ever did," said Michael.

They all paused to shoot him a look like he was mad, before continuing to argue—all except Tom, who walked silently to the railing like a forlorn wife on a widow's watch. He glared out to sea, hoping against hope for his innocence to return, secretly knowing it never would, just like the widow's husband lost to the depths.

***

"Even if we don't go after it, it could come back for us," said Michael, sure that it would.

It ate my great-grandfather, and now it wants me, he thought.

"Yeah, that's right, we might not have to do anything at all," said Little T with a manic smile, a huge bead of sweat dripping down the side of his face. His tongue darted out to lap it up like that of a honeyeater.

"It's bloody gone, whatever it is," said Pricey.

"Still, nothing wrong with being ready if it does come," said Jords, turning a full circle, knife held out defensively before him, as if the megalodon would leap over the side of the boat any moment, and he would be locked in single combat with it.

"Let's get the rest of the fish below, and all this blood and guts cleared up," said Pricey. "Then we can indulge in these damn fairy tales."

"You still don't believe it was a megalodon?" said Michael. "Here, look at this." He pointed over the side. There was a dead shark floating in the water—well, half a shark—bit clean through the mid-section.

Pricey shrugged as if he'd seen it all before.

"Work," he said simply.

"And who made you captain?" asked Jords.

"Jords, how long we going to play this damn game?" said Pricey, bending to pick up a tub, putting it between him and the knife-wielding maniac like a shield.

Jords shook his head, the knife shaking with it, flashing silver like a swimming fish. "I've served my time, and the captain said I was in charge if he wasn't here."

"I'm in charge!" bellowed a voice from the cabin. Calvin emerged like a bear from hibernation, hair scruffy, eyes bleary. His halitosis heralded his presence, going before him, an invisible miasma of stink which brought them all to their knees like servants before their sovereign lord. "And what's all this I hear about a megalodon?"

***

They braced themselves for the return of the megalodon like warriors on the eve of a battle. But the tension melted into boredom after the last of the fish were packed on ice in the freezer below decks. There was nothing to do but wait... and drink.

Michael watched them all sullenly as the crew lit up cigarettes to accompany their drinks, and Calvin even produced a pipe, which he packed heartily with tobacco and lit, and then puffed away happily like a grandfather doting on his grandchildren.

"The megalodon is a subject dear to the hearts of old fishermen everywhere," said the captain.

"I'm an old fisherman," said Pricey with crossed arms.

Calvin ignored him, continuing. "It represents the pinnacle of fishing skill and achievement, the ultimate in man versus beast. To catch a megalodon is to be a living legend."

"Or a dead one, more like," muttered Michael.

"Oh, yeah, you reckon your great-grandfather caught one, don't you?"

"More like it caught him."

"He proved unworthy."

"And you think you're equal to the task? It'll kill you, too. And all of us, if you insist on going after it."

Calvin smiled wanly, which turned into a grimace as he clutched his sore head. "What's life for if not to reach after greatness?"

"Going home alive," said Tom sullenly.

"He doesn't want you risking his inheritance," Jords sneered.

"As if you're keen for the thing to come back," said Michael. "Going to stab it with your knife, are you?"

"I'll fucking stab you if you like."

"No one is stabbing anyone," said Calvin.

"Can you take his knife away then?" said Michael.

Calvin looked at him with astonishment. "Take away a fisherman's knife? I've never heard of such a thing."

"Something bad is going to happen."

"Fishing is a dangerous game. If you don't like it, you can get off my boat."

"And go where, exactly?"

Calvin shrugged. "Land."

"Not a lot of land hereabouts."

"You wanted on the boat. You're on the boat. This is the boat. This is the life."

"We've caught the fish. Now that we know there's a megalodon out here we should call it a win and head in."

"Fuck, and here I was thinking it was Jords who wanted to stab me in the back, take my boat."

"We've not caught enough yet," said Pricey earnestly. "The captain has to make a profit and we need to get paid."

"Think of what we'll get for a megalodon," said Little T. He had the look of a man lost to gold rush fever, his eyes glassy, envisioning the treasure to be had.

"We'll get nothing but some giant jaws snapping down on our necks," said Michael, vividly reliving the story of his great-grandfather in his mind.

Little T shuddered with pleasure fear. "That would be good, too."

"Okay, you're nuts."

"We're all a little nuts," said Calvin. "Or we wouldn't be here."

"I'm not nuts. I just want to fish and make an honest living," said Pricey.

"Yes," said Calvin, slapping his knee and lurching to his feet. "To fish. That's exactly where we need to go."

"So we're going to get back to work?" said Pricey hopefully.

"No fish, no guts. No guts, no sharks."

Pricey deflated. "Oh."

"You've heard of two birds, one stone. Well, here we have a case of two fish, one hook."

"Or two sharks, one hook," said Little T, rubbing his meaty hands together.

"Thankfully there's only one out there," said Michael.

***

"So, we hunt the megalodon by doing what we normally do, track down schools of fish?" asked Michael.

"Yeah," said Tom, rolling his eyes. "It's the drink talking. He doesn't even think there's a megalodon out here."

"But you saw it. It's definitely out here."

"Don't remind me, or I'll turn this boat around and head home right now."

"Why don't you?"

"Because this is the only future I've got."

"So you're just waiting on your inheritance?"

"I'm working for my inheritance."

"My dad didn't give me shit. One day he took off, didn't look back."

"You think my dad is giving me anything? I work hard. I'm paying for this."

And maybe with my life, thought Tom.

It was just the two of them, he and Michael, up on the dog shift at the helm, trying to find a shoal of fish in the middle of the night using the instruments. So far, they'd had little luck in shooting for a mark.

"You may as well go get some sleep," Tom said.

"I'm trying to learn how all this works," said Michael.

"According to my dad I don't know anything anyway."

"You're literally piloting the boat while everyone else sleeps off their drink."

Tom gently adjusted the steering wheel, an archaic wooden one with spokes. "Easy enough when there's nothing out here to run into."

"What about all these beeping instruments?"

"Sonar, water temp, depth sounder," said Tom, pointing at the various screens. "Weather radar."

"And how do you know where the fish are?"

"I'm working a grid of the map, heading back and forth. I box off an area, tick it off the list. If there's any fish, they'll show up on the readings. It's like casting an electronic line, seeing what you get. We call it 'shooting the way.'"

"You think you'll find something tonight?" said Michael, peering at the glowing green screens.

Tom squinted into the dark night through the windshield, waves breaking over the bow. "Let's hope so. The sooner the holds are full, the sooner we can go home and get paid."

"You sound keen for this to be over."

"With the megalodon out here, yeah, I am."

"But this is your whole life. You get back, unload, and come back out again."

Tom snorted. "That's the nature of work, isn't it? It never ends. No different than that factory."

"Yeah, maybe that wasn't as bad as I thought after all. At least we got to go to bed at night."

"I said you can go to sleep."

"You sure you'll be alright?" asked Michael, stretching his arms and yawning.

Tom yawned, a contagious response. "Don't do that. Better flick on the coffee machine as you go."

Michael went to the head of the stairs, turned back. "Your dad is lucky to have you, you know. You do more work than the rest of those bastards."

"Little T and Pricey are alright."

"Not Jords?"

"Fuck that guy."

They both laughed.

"But really," said Michael. "Your dad should treat you better."

"He's trying to toughen me up, prepare me for this life."

"Maybe he should try toughening himself up, because it seems like this life is too much for him."

"Mum died," said Tom with a shrug, as if this explained everything.

***

When Calvin woke up, his whole world was spinning. Around and around went his head, the motion descending into his guts, stirring up the foul brew there, agitating it unpleasantly. He threw up a little in his mouth, but swallowed it to remind himself he was still alive. It tasted like gory entrails. He grunted in disgust, wiped his mouth with the back of his hand, and felt the slick moisture there. He looked at the mess, realised with a start that it was red, that there was blood on his hands.

He sat up straight, the heaving motion pumping his drink-abused stomach like a bellows. The pressure erupted up his gullet, out his open, gaping mouth like a volcano blowing its top. The ceiling was peppered explosively with dark matter. Hot gases stunk up the room as red lava bile slid viscously down the mountainside of his monstrous gut.

"Fucking hell," said Pricey, springing to his feet like a cat stepped on in its sleep. Bouncing off the ceiling and somehow landing on his feet, he looked down at himself in horror. He—like Jords and Little T, who had not been roused from the depths of their grog comas by the spewing sounds—was covered in blood-coloured bile. The two sleeping men rolled over in this putrid filth, the contents of the captain's stomach sloshing around the floor like seawater in the bilges.

With the red colouring of the stuff, and the rotten egg smell, it was as if a demonic poltergeist had swooped through the cabin, leaving behind a sticky ectoplasm which coated every surface—the captain certainly looked pale enough to be a ghost. He peered blearily at the unholy scene around him, now not so sure he was still alive. The pungent, sulphurous heat of the close air reminded him of hell, and he felt like death warmed up.

He turned his head, trying to make more sense of things. It was a mistake. The slight movement triggered a delicate switch in his brain, leading to an internal cascade of neurons tumbling like dominoes. He made a sick belching sound, felt the volcano burbling away once more deep inside, ready for an explosive round two.

Pricey saw this as he was shaking himself off in disgust. His face went slack in dawning horror, the dark rings under his eyes dragged down into sagging ovals.

"Oh, God, please, don't," he said, rushing forward with hand outstretched, as if he might reach the ticking time bomb and defuse it before it went off. He moved in slow motion, a man moving sluggishly underwater, seeking to outrun some terrifying monster in a dream, but unable to do so. Though he managed to close the short distance in that infinitely stretching time—even clamping his fingers on Calvin's lips, pinching them closed with all his desperate strength—the forces seeking to escape were too much. He was rewarded with a shotgun blast full to the face as the captain exploded once more. A percussive bark of spew threw Pricey back, his mouth full of the captain's vomit. He stumbled and tripped on his sleeping crewmates, and fell hard on his arse. Spluttering like a drowning man, he wrenched his fingers into his mouth to scoop out the filth, shaking his head to try and clear it from his eyes. His feet tap-danced like a hanged man's, kicking Little T and Jords, who both finally woke up and immediately wished they hadn't.

***

The spinning sensation continued even as Calvin gathered up the shattered fragments of his reality. It was accompanied by a familiar humming which reverberated through the whole boat, continuing into the nerve fibres of his body as if the two were one. There was a shrill quality to it, like a high-pitched warning cry.

"You hear that?" said Pricey, his big ears twitching. Concern wrinkled his weathered face. He headed towards the door, and not just to escape the miasma of filth.

Calvin nodded to himself, frowning in an effort to think. He knew that sound. It was the boat's engine over-revving. A glance out a porthole revealed clouds gliding by like silhouetted images, white ink blots on a blue background, the shapes containing some hidden subconscious message he was too numb to yet interpret with anything more than intuitive alarm.

"Something's wrong," said Calvin, stomping over Little T and Jords. The two men picked themselves up as if from the bottom of a muddy bomb crater. They were looking around at each other like the miraculous survivors of a disastrous defeat on the battlefield.

"Whose blood is this?" asked Jords, indicating first the wall, then the floor, and finally himself. He had a look on his face as if he had been witness to some violent crime, but his shocked outrage was tempered by the confusion that perhaps he was the one who had been stabbed and would soon die in a pool of his own blood, and that he was still too drunk to realise it or feel the pain.

"It's red wine barf," said Little T, squeezing his eyes shut as if trying to blot out the rancid stink by not acknowledging it.

"But we don't have any red wine."

"Not any more we don't."

"I'll never drink again," said Jords. It was a lie, but one he believed in the moment. He tried to get clear of the sick mess, slipping and sliding as if on a deck awash during a storm. Hand over hand, bracing himself, he made his way topside, the stairs slick with vomit. Little T didn't bother to follow. He was somewhere, anywhere else. He sat hunched on a seat like a meditative Buddha, and tried to think of nothing.

***

Calvin's bulk, amorphous and globular, extruded out of the cabin door like paste from a tube. He floated uneasily with the motion of the ship, an overfull balloon in threat of being popped by Pricey's sharp, poking arms as they indicated this and that with frantic gestures. First there was the sea, gliding past them at a furious pace, churned into a huge wash of white water in their wake. Then there was the boat itself, the deck skewed at a steep angle left to right, the starboard rail down near the waterline, the port side hanging in the air. Finally, there was something even more obtuse, a figure balled up tight in a corner, oblivious to it all, swaying in the shade of the awning like a human cocoon.

"And what the hell do you think you're doing?" said Calvin, infuriated by the sight of the man in the hammock. He gave the bundle of canvas a kick. A head popped out, hair tousled, eyes mere slits. It was Michael.

"You're meant to be on watch!" growled Calvin. He shook the hammock like an enraged ape shaking a banana tree. Michael tumbled out onto the deck, all elbows and knees, banging each of them hard with cries of protest.

"Tom told me to get some sleep," he said. "He's on the helm."

"The fucking boat is out of control." Calvin swooped his arm around like a slingshot to both indicate the dizzying spin of the horizon and also the hard-over path of the boat, steering in an endless circle. The movement sent a wave of nausea through him, but his guts were now nothing but an empty barrel, and he only dry retched. Still, it felt like someone had punched him in the stomach. The fist of pain remained there, a product of his growing alarm and concern for the boat as he gripped the hand railing of the ladder up to the bridge.

"I'm going to wring his fucking neck when I get a hold of him," he said, struggling and panting with each rung. The effort and discomfort he felt was going to come out of Tom's hide.

"And the fuel out of his pay," he said, finishing the sentiment out loud. He glanced back at the motors, screaming as they used up the precious resource at a prodigious rate.

A quick sweep of the bridge revealed nothing but a steering wheel turned over on hard lock to starboard, the throttle pushed all the way forward. "Where the fuck is that bloody kid?" said Calvin, righting the wheel and easing back on the gas.

"Do you think he got drunk, fell asleep?" asked Pricey, coming up behind. He glanced behind the chair at the helm in search of Tom there, passed out. Calvin winced. The words were a needle, jabbing at his soul as much as at his raw brain, sore with the pounding headache of his hangover.

"What are you trying to say, that I don't have the right to unwind with a drink after a long day?" Calvin said to Pricey, who frowned in confusion.

"No..." Pricey said. "Though we often go a bit overboard and—"

"So you *are* blaming me. I won't stand for it, not on my own ship." Calvin swayed, thought discretion the better part of valour, and fell into a chair, the leather wheezing in protest. He waved a dismissive hand at Pricey. "Now go find the boy and get him to explain this mess." Calvin looked at the fuel gauge. His eyes bulged out of their sockets to see it so low. "Fucking hell, it must have been running like this all night. We'll be lucky to limp back to Darwin on this lot."

"We've got reserves," said Pricey. "The jerry cans in the hold."

"I know that. They're the only thing standing between us and being stranded out here. We'll need them soon enough." As if to illustrate the point, the engines sputtered and cut out, trailing smoke as they burned up the last coughs of fumes. "See? Fetch them when you fetch my useless lump of a son, will you?"

"Something might have happened to the little shit," said Jords, his head appearing at the top of the ladder.

"Don't say that," said Pricey, clucking his tongue.

Jords leaned back on the ladder, peered around, his long nose looking like a weather vane catching a turning wind. "I mean, I don't see him anywhere, and it's not like it's the biggest boat in the world."

"He's hiding because he knows I'll cane the skin off his back for this," said Calvin.

"And what has he done, exactly? Why would he pull the boat into a spin, rev the engines, and then abandon his post?" asked Pricey, not unreasonably.

Calvin tapped a finger against his lips thoughtfully, tasted the filth caking them. He grimaced, looked at his hands again, and saw the red wine puke staining his fingernails like blood.

Pricey has a point, thought Calvin, but the real question was the one posed by Jords. *Could something have happened to Tom?*

The captain spun in the seat, looked at the instruments on the boat's dashboard, turning to them for direction as he had for decades, his whole life at sea guided by these auguries. Their pings and flashing dots, numbers and graphs—these were his only gods, besides the drink—and they never failed him.

Just as they didn't fail him now.

"Fucking hell, Tom's only gone and found us the mother lode!" he said, seeing the massive signatures which indicated the presence of a huge shoal of fish. They were right beneath the boat, ready to be plucked from the sea like ripe grapes from the vine.

Pricey came and looked, eyes sparkling, dollar signs clouding his vision as they had already done for Calvin. Behind them, Jords leant from the ladder, threw out a hand with his head tilted back, and howled like a pirate at the top of a wooden mast having sighted a fat prize vessel on the horizon. No one paid much mind to Michael as he asked where Tom was, where it was he could possibly be. The other crew were too excited—so excited, in fact, that they missed another, much more ominous blip on the sonar, closing in on the shoal of fish, and on them.

***

Greed didn't cure the hangovers of the crew, but it distracted them enough to endure the work that needed doing. If anyone besides Michael missed Tom, it was only because this was the kind of work they liked to foist onto him. Jords and Pricey grumbled about the boy not doing his share. Whether it was through him shirking or because of some more sinister fate didn't matter much to them—they were still stuck working harder than they liked. Mucking in besides them, Little T and Michael went about their duties in silence, each locked up with their thoughts of the future, the former excited and terrified, the latter simply terrified.

Calvin watched them work with a pensive attitude, trying to calculate the weight of fish they were taking on versus the fuel they had left, judging the correct tipping point when avarice would turn into suicide. If he thought of his son, it was only because Michael, stripped to the waist and hauling on wet ropes, reminded him of the boy, or perhaps of his own lost youth. He closed his eyes to stop the needles of light jabbing his brain through his eye sockets, or perhaps to prevent the awful truth of Tom's absence wheedling its way into his calculations. He hardly needed the boy's life placed on those delicate scales. Nursing his gargantuan head in his hands like a fragile egg, he laboriously went over the numbers again.

"Little T, go check the fuel reserves in the hold," he said.

"I've already been down," said Little T. "You know what's there."

And what's not there, thought Little T, but said nothing, his face wrinkling with the effort of holding his tongue.

"Head below, and get that look off your face already," snapped Calvin, trying not to move his eyeballs in his closed lids. It felt like they were attached to strings in his brain, and each movement tugged at something unpleasant he would sooner ignore.

"What look?" said Little T with a shrug, his face softening like kneaded dough, transforming back into the ready mask of affability he always wore.

"Tom's not down there," whispered Michael.

"I know that," said Little T out of the side of a smile which didn't reach his eyes.

"Then where is he?"

Little T swept a hand across the horizon of the sea. "Where else is there to go?"

"Why aren't these idiots doing anything about it?"

"I think you can see why."

The net burst open and the fish spilled onto the deck like the guts of a giant sea monster after a feeding frenzy.

"Calvin cares more about fish and money than his own son?" hissed Michael. He grabbed Little T by the arm with a desperate grip and gave him a shake. Little T swatted at the hand like it was an annoying fly.

Michael didn't let go, his fingers pressing white into the flesh. "If he's lost at sea, we need to call the federal police, start a search," he urged. "Hell, we need to at least look for him ourselves."

"And leave all this behind?" said Little T sardonically. He gave a mirthless laugh. "Tom wouldn't be the first to go over the side. And he won't be the last, either, if you catch my drift, so best to leave it alone, cuzzie."

"But why doesn't Calvin even give a shit?"

They both looked at Calvin, sitting like a bloated frog on the chair at the helm, swivelling back and forth, his mind unfathomable behind closed eyes.

"He's blind to it," said Little T. "He can't face reality."

"It's our job to make him face it," said Michael.

Little T used his own meaty paw to unclench Michael's hand, peel it off as if it were a tenacious spider. He glanced at the rest of the crew meaningfully, as if to draw Michael's attention to the invisible strands of a complex web. Jords was eying them as if they were turds under his boots, his knife flickering in the sunlight as he worked—its brilliant flashing was a wink and a promise of violence turned upon any who stood in the way of his meal ticket. Pricey didn't look their way at all, busy worshiping at the altar of the horde of fish, muscles straining at the ropes, eyes catching the sun with the glint of coins.

"Get back to work, alright?" said Little T. He gave Michael back his hand as if it were a gift, a solemn piece of wise advice for him to cherish. "There's more than one way to meet your end on a fishing trawler, and the captain has the sharks circling."

***

Even as the fishermen tightened their nets and drew in their catch, rubbing their hands together with triumphal avarice, another hunter was closing in, its net cast wider for a bigger catch. Having herded the shoal of fish together, the megalodon knew the humans would come, the bait irresistible to them. To it, their vessel was nothing more than another type of bloated sea creature, one which was inedible, yet possessed of a peculiar and useful ability: turning the fish it gathered inside out, consuming the flesh but dumping the guts into the sea. And with this offering of blood, the megalodon's prey— the lesser sharks of the ocean—would lock on to this location.

Then the real slaughter would begin.

***

"Why do I have to do this bloody grunt work?" complained Jords, his Bowie knife too big and clumsy for the delicate work of gutting fish. Yet it was as if his fist could not relinquish the weapon, like he knew it was the source of all his power, his one bargaining chip, a trump card he held in reserve to play in an emergency.

"You're hacking at that damned fish, there'll be nothing left soon," said Pricey, similarly chagrined to be on gutting duty. The captain insisted they all pitch in, for they had taken a prodigious haul out of the sea and the deck strained with the massive weight of fish. This didn't mean that Calvin himself condescended to do any of the gutting, but he did stay and supervise, pacing the deck. He took slugs from a bottle he used like a marshal's baton, directing his troops in battle, growing more bellicose the drunker he got. Little T and Michael were just as unwilling in their work, sensing if they did too good a job they would provide Jords and Pricey with an excuse to slack off.

For each of the crew it felt like they were compensating for the conspicuous absence of Tom without the tacit acknowledgement of the young man's ghost hanging over them like a pall. With their busyness with the fish, it seemed that Jords, Pricey, and Calvin had silently agreed on the plausible deniability of their case, that Tom was in hiding to avoid the consequences of his negligence. Michael and Little T were powerless to make them face the grim reality no one wanted to face.

"He'll not be getting a share of this haul, either," said Calvin.

The crew knew he was too far gone with greed and drink to see any sense, and this lifted the burden of guilt from the shoulders of every man on deck, knowing it wasn't their call to go look for Tom, and not their son who was missing anyway. They could collect their own share of the fish money—now increased with Tom cut out—with a clear conscience.

Not that Michael thought of it that way. He felt a distance growing between even he and Little T, who, though wiser in the ways of the sea and fishing trawlers than Michael, seemed just as complicit in a murder by proxy—one of neglect, abuse, and the uncaring economy of the sea.

Michael took a load of guts to the side of the ship and dumped them over. Turning back for another load, he found Calvin looming over him like a mountainous shadow, his bulk blocking out the sun, forming a grotesque halo around his huge, bulbous head.

"You think I've forgotten him, don't you?" he said darkly, his tone low and sonorous, crushing like the depths of the ocean.

"I think we need to look for him," said Michael. His voice broke nervously in a way he wasn't happy with.

Calvin leaned in closer, revealing the sun. It shone in Michael's face like the flashlight of an interrogator. Calvin's face was now even deeper in shadow by contrast.

"He'll come to us," said the captain ominously, a soothsayer foretelling the future.

"And what does that mean?"

"The megalodon is coming."

"I thought you meant Tom."

"These little fish," said Calvin, jerking a thumb over his shoulder, to either mean the dead fish on the deck, or perhaps the human crew. "They mean nothing."

"I thought you were in it for the money."

"Money, like human life, is for spending. You think this is my first crew?"

"So you'll sacrifice us? And for what: a chance at the big time, to become a legend?"

"I'm already a legend. I'm a story, told over and over in your head, which you mistake for a life lived. It's an illusion."

Calvin straightened, and yet his shadowy face still had no features, only the outline of a fat head.

"That's the drink talking," said Michael. "I had my own problems, you know it. Reality can bend under the weight of an addiction. But with willpower, you can bend it back, see things straight again."

Calvin growled like a cornered animal. "I have no choice. No one does. That's the only thing the sea has taught me. I go where it takes me."

"Even if that's into the jaws of the megalodon?"

"It's either him or us."

"And what about Tom?"

"Funny thing is, I can't seem to picture his face," said Calvin wistfully, staring into the clouds like he might see his son in them. "It's like he's a memory that's already fading, seen through the opaque glass of a bottle."

He lifted his grog to eye level. The liquid inside the bottle caught the sun, looking sea green in the glass. A little piece of cork floated on the surface of the booze, jostled by waves as Calvin shook the bottle like an angry god.

"You don't think I would save my own son if I could?" he said bitterly, spittle flying like orange sparks in the sunlight. "I can't even save myself, God damn it!"

"We've got enough fish. We could go home," pleaded Michael. He, too, was quickly forgetting Tom, now concerned for his own welfare as he realised, with growing certainty, that the captain was steering them to their doom.

Calvin shook his head, knowing what Michael didn't, that their doom had come to meet them, was already there in the water, encircling them, closing like a noose around their necks as the sharks gathered for the feast.

***

Frenzied biting made a sound like gunfire. Flashing, razor sharp teeth were drawn swords, stabbing into flesh. Grey bodies heaved in their masses, locked in mortal combat. A mighty war cry rose up, a roar produced not by mouths but by the movement of powerful fins slicing the water. Gore in the sea was churned to pink foam. The dead floated in great banks of burst flesh, trailing strings of entrails like the tentacles of hundreds of jellyfish.

This was a primordial clash of arms, a glimpse into a prehistoric past before the time of man, when mighty monsters ruled land and sea, and the weak died and were consumed.

Calvin watched the battle of shark versus shark unfold from the deck of the fishing trawler. He was like a general witnessing a Pyrrhic victory, well aware the glory of this moment would fade and all that would be left afterwards would be the butcher's bill, haunting his dreams, where even the drink couldn't block the truth from bubbling up from the subconscious depths of his mind. Already he knew the cost was too high, for to witness this fight was to watch Armageddon, oblivion the only outcome for all involved. This was a fight to the death.

The conflict was not an even one, a single mighty hero versus an impossible horde. The megalodon reared out of the water like a leviathan as it chomped and swallowed the lesser sharks in their multitudes. Not that it was getting things all its own way. In return it was bleeding down its flanks, great gouged wounds carved into its scarred hide by vicious and desperate opponents. But these were but bee stings to a giant, and could only annoy and slow down the megalodon, not destroy it. To Calvin, it seemed almost obscene that such haughty kings of the sea—great whites and tiger sharks—should be humbled by their real master.

"There's always something bigger," he said to himself, glancing derisively over his shoulder at his crew, his own lesser shadows. They stood in a huddled mass, watching the megalodon in mute horror, or rapt fascination, or glittering avarice—perhaps all of these at once, such was the befuddled complexity of the human condition when confronted with something so powerful, yet so impossible, as a megalodon. Myth touched their minds in strange ways, though predictably Jords had his knife out in front of him, jabbing the air like a spectator at a boxing match miming the actions of the real fighters.

Calvin ignored them for now. They were pawns and they would have their time to be moved. Instead he attempted to savour the rarest of sights—a prehistoric beast brought back from the realms of extinction for one last show of gladiatorial combat. It was a spectacle to remember for the rest of his life. He smiled wanly, keenly aware the rest of his life might not be very long, for he and his crew weren't spectators at all, but combatants themselves, and he was about to throw them into the arena.

***

"Ready the nets!" he shouted, startling the crew. They jumped as if the megalodon had launched itself at the boat.

No such luck, thought Calvin. *Instead, we have to go to it.*

"What are we doing with the nets?" asked Pricey. The man was still in shock from the reality of the megalodon being revealed in all its awesome, and colossally large, glory.

"We're going to catch us a shark," said Little T with gnomish glee.

"Or it's going to catch us," said Michael.

A tremor ran through Little T's stout frame, like a thick tree in a strong wind. "Stop, I'm already as hard as I can get."

"No shark is going to eat me," said Jords, thrusting at the air with his knife. "I'll shove this right up its arsehole."

"I'll feed you to it myself if I get half a chance," muttered Calvin to himself as he climbed the ladder, sat himself at the helm.

"You're not seriously going to try to net that thing are you?" Pricey shouted through cupped hands. The only answer he got was Calvin throttling up the engines and steering the prow straight at the heart of the seething cauldron of battle.

"Oh, fuck it," said Pricey to himself, then to the rest of the crew, as if it was his idea and he retained some shred of authority, "Ready the nets!"

The others didn't need to be told. They were already hard at it. It was clear to all now that it was either do their job, and do it well, or die. One glimpse at the massive megalodon, tearing its way through the final shiver of sharks, told them that much.

Calvin had never understood why a group of sharks was called a shiver. He did now, recalling a time when even a single great white was enough to send a shiver of fear down his spine. That was a long time ago, the years spanned by an ocean of blood and death that had tempered and hardened his soul. Now his fear was not that a single shark lay before him, but that there were hundreds—monsters, every one of them—now dead, slain by the granddaddy of them all. To stand at the top of the food chain was an illusion easily shattered.

There's always something bigger, repeated Calvin in his mind.

"Megalodon," he said through gritted teeth, as if to banish the monster through naming it. The word felt hot on his tongue, a curse word, tasting bitter, and he spat it out, this time at greater volume, a bellowed war shout to steel his courage. "Megalodon!"

He gunned the engines, charging the boat into the fray.

***

"He's going to get us killed," said Pricey, referring more to the speed with which the captain was taking the boat in, rather than the monster they were heading towards.

"And when was that ever in doubt?" said Little T, smiling, at peace with himself, his glistening eyes not leaving the megalodon for one moment.

"This was meant to be my way out," said Michael, lamenting ever setting foot on this cursed boat.

"There's no escaping your past," said Jords, glancing over his shoulder, as if he would find a line of his victims there, waiting their turn to kick his teeth in.

"He's heading straight for that monster. How we meant to get the nets ready in time?" said Pricey, working as hard as three men, desperate to get the nets in place. They were bearing down on the megalodon as it finished its feeding frenzy, the distance closing fast.

"I don't think he's going to stop," said Michael, glancing at the monster rearing up in the water, then at the back of the captain's head. "We're on a collision course."

"A what?" said Pricey in disbelief.

"He's going to ram the fucking thing!" said Michael. "Brace yourselves!"

But no sooner had those words escaped his lips than the trawler collided with the megalodon head on, nose on nose. There was a colossal bang of impact, the crew thrown forward, sprawling. They rattled about the deck like ball bearings, their brains shaken loose. In the immediate aftermath of pain and confusion, it wasn't clear who had come off worse, the boat or the beast.

***

"Okay, have you got those nets ready?" said Calvin, as if it wasn't clear enough the answer was no by the fact the crew were scattered across the deck, half unconscious. He slid down the ladder, went to the ropes himself, and hauled the nets off the side of the boat using the outriggers so that they hung over the sea.

"Are we dead?" asked Michael, sure the boat must now be sinking, the hull as shattered by the collision as he was. It was with a shock he looked around, found everything in disarray, yet the boat itself was not smashed to pieces.

"Where's my knife? Who's got my knife?" said Jords.

"I think I caught it," said Pricey. He held up a hand, but the knife wasn't in it. Instead, it was buried up to the hilt in his forearm.

"Well, give it back."

"You fucking psycho," said Michael. Aching and disorientated, he rummaged around in the debris on deck in search of the first aid kit. He found the old, battered tackle box it had been stored in, though it was smashed open, the contents scattered. Michael sighed, but secretly he was pleased for the distraction as he tried to locate the bandages and rubbing alcohol. It took his mind off the rasping sound he heard, deafeningly loud, like a giant gnawing on a bone.

"Forget that shit," said Calvin. "We've got to catch the megalodon while it's stunned."

"I don't think we stunned it," said Little T, leaning over the railing to look down the length of the boat. "It's chomping on the hull."

A thunderclap of sound was accompanied by a blur of movement like a bright flash of lightning. Michael blinked once in reflex, the scene changing in that split second. One moment Little T was at the side of the boat. The next, all that was left of him was a smear of blood along the railing. Michael was screaming before his conscious mind realised what had happened.

"Shut up, you fucking idiot," said Calvin, giving Michael a boot up the butt that sent him over face first. The impact of the deck was a stinging blow to the head, and he sprung up, humiliated and ready to fight, but Pricey was there, putting himself between Michael and the captain. His face had drained of colour, and his voice shook as he spoke.

"You want to do something to help, grab a rope, or you'll join Little T as shark food," he said to Michael. Sweat was pouring down his forehead as he clutched his impaled arm with his good hand.

Michael couldn't tell if that was a threat or merely stating facts. The conviction behind it was unmistakable, though. He decided the best thing to do was not argue with the man with a Bowie knife through his arm, so he jumped on a rope with Jords, who was snarling like a beast as he pulled, his pointed little rat teeth showing.

The nets fanned out across the water, boxing in the megalodon, who turned at bay to attack its tormentors.

***

"Yes, yes, that's got him!" shouted Calvin with enthusiasm, abandoning his line and running for the ladder to the bridge. Michael didn't share the captain's excitement. To him, it seemed the boat was sinking, and rather than having caught the megalodon, it had caught them. The net that successfully snared the monster was now an anchor dragging the boat down into the water.

Michael heard the engines first chugging to life and then screaming at high pitch as Calvin gunned the throttle, pitting the powerful engines against the might of the beast. At first, it seemed there was little difference, no gains to be had, but slowly, surely, machine won out against nature. The boat surged ahead and the megalodon was brought to the surface and dragged behind the boat, its fins pinned and useless in the tangled mass of netting.

***

The creature was impossibly large for a shark, filling a net capable of catching a whole school of fish. The outrigger beams bent like fishing poles and the winches and pulleys shrieked for grease to ease their efforts as they hauled at the monster, trying to get it clear of the water. Michael wasn't sure the fishing trawler was big enough for the task. It was already low in the water, overburdened with their catch of fish, and this extra weight took it dangerously down to the waterline. There was a real risk they would soon be awash.

It wasn't helping that the megalodon was still putting up a hell of a fight, squirming and flailing about so that the boat rocked as if in a storm. But the mighty struggles of the megalodon also tangled it further and wore it out. The netting cut deeply into its flesh, blood trailing in the wake of the boat as the captain continued to gun the engines in an effort to exhaust the beast. Smaller sharks followed along behind, drawn by the scent of blood, or otherwise to witness the humiliating defeat of their predator. They cavorted like dolphins to see the great one laid low.

Pricey—ignoring his wound or seeking vengeance for it—worked the winch one-handed, hauling the huge creature from the sea as the captain finally pulled the boat up to conserve fuel. He locked the winch with a clunk, the megalodon up against the boat's side, as the engines cut out.

The crew gathered at the railing like men at a sea burial, solemn and silent, looking down at the deadly monster. The thing was near equal to their boat in length, its gills flapping as if panting in exhaustion, the jaw moving without sound, impotently chomping at the netting. An eerie feeling washed in across the empty sea like a breeze, sending a tingle down Michael's back. He suddenly, out of nowhere, really wanted a smoke, and sweat broke out on his lower back as his hands began to tremble. He closed his eyes as a means to escape, but waiting for him in the dark was a vision of Little T's face, so his eyelids snapped open and fixated on the single upwards turned eye of the megalodon. It looked intelligent and in pain, and Michael felt sick with himself for having been a part of this. Small waves lapped against the hull as the great whites gathered around to bite chunks out of the megalodon.

"Let's get the thing out of the water before those bastards steal our prize," said Calvin in disdain.

Grim faced and bent over with pain, Pricey hit the winch once more like an executioner activating a guillotine. The screaming of the machine was the shrill cry of the slaughtered, the only one to be heard as the megalodon went silently to its death.

Or so the crew thought, not aware the wounded megalodon emitted a sound beyond their senses—an ultrasonic frequency sonar distress cry that could only be heard by one of its own.

***

"I would gut the bloody thing, but you've still got my knife," Jords said to Pricey with a manic laugh. He stepped back to avoid the thrashing tail of the megalodon they had dumped on the deck, nearly filling the entire space with its curled up bulk.

"Anyone think this megalodon isn't as big as the first one we saw?" asked Michael, scampering up the ladder to the bridge, wanting to be well clear of the thing. Despite being trussed up in the net like a roast turkey, the megalodon was putting up a fight, and it wasn't at all clear how they were going to kill it.

The answer was soon in coming, a deafening pair of bangs slapping percussively against Michael's eardrums, nearly knocking him from the ladder and into the waiting jaws of the monster. He clung on for dear life, head spinning and ears still ringing loudly.

Calvin stood over him with a shotgun, smiling like a lunatic as smoke drifted up past his face. For a second Michael thought he himself had been shot, but knew this couldn't be the case. Still, he couldn't work out another possible explanation until, with casual ease, Calvin broke the weapon open, loaded two more plump red cartridges into the double breaches. Lifting the shotgun to fire, Michael followed the aim over his own shoulder, saw that the previous two shots had blasted a pair of ugly holes up the back of the megalodon to match the chunks taken out of it by the great whites. Calvin corrected his aim, swaying only slightly, and pulped that huge intelligent eye to jelly with his next shot. The fourth he put through the same place, penetrating deep into its brain.

The megalodon didn't die immediately. Instead, it shuddered spasmodically like a man having a fit.

Michael's heart broke even as he willed the thing to die. Finally, with a thud, it collapsed on the deck like a dropped jellyfish, its mass spreading out, a deflated sack of flesh. With a similar sequence, Pricey, standing by the winch with blood streaming from his arm, shook, stumbled, and finally fell, an old oak in the forest brought low by a brutal world.

"Wait, no," said Michael, not wanting this to happen, but helpless to prevent it. There was nothing he could do but stretch out a hand uselessly as Pricey tumbled backwards. He fell over the railing and into the waiting mouths of the hungry pack of great whites gathered there.

***

"He's gone and lost my good fucking knife, hasn't he," said Jords, peering over the edge of the boat, searching the water as if the knife would miraculously float to the surface.

"You heartless bastard. You killed him, you know that, right?" said Michael, giving him a push.

"Hey, hey, watch it." Jords had to pull back hard to prevent himself going over into the drink, where the great whites gathered menacingly, waiting for a second course.

"Jords didn't kill him," said Calvin, joining them at the railing, his shotgun broken open and held in the crook of his arm, as if he were an English gentleman out for a pleasant day of pheasant hunting. "The megalodon killed him."

"It was *his* knife," said Michael.

"And if I had it right now I'd gut you," said Jords.

"Exactly, without that blade you're not such a big man, are you?"

"Tsk, tsk," said Calvin. "Careful now, there are plenty more knives on board. Speaking of, why don't you go run and grab one, boy?"

Michael's voice squeaked in horror as he said, "You're not going to let him gut me, are you?"

Jords looked to the captain for confirmation, smiling with his wicked rat teeth.

"No," said Calvin, jerking his fat head to send Jords on his way. "I want him to gut the megalodon. It's weighing us down and I need to clear some of its bulk."

"What about Pricey?"

"He's dead, you little turd. And if I wasn't suddenly so short on crew I'd send you over to join him. This might not surprise you, but I don't exactly like you."

Calvin stroked the shotgun affectionately like a pet cat as they waited for Jords to return.

"Found a plenty good one and all," said Jords, holding up the biggest knife Michael had ever seen.

"Alright, give it to Michael, he can have the honour," said Calvin.

Jords reluctantly relinquished the blade. With the cold steel heavy in his hand, Michael considered stabbing the pair of them—or at least Calvin, for being such a callous bastard. He didn't even care if it didn't kill him, just wanted him to feel pain, to know he wasn't above all this, but connected, causing it.

Instead, his hand fell by his side, the knife pointed at the deck. He turned to the megalodon, the last thing on this ship he wanted to stab, but it was the only thing upon which to take out his rage. Before Calvin and Jords could get themselves clear, Michael rammed the blade underhanded into the belly of the beast. The knife sunk to the hilt in the thick fat of the megalodon and, with an anguished cry, wishing to be anywhere but here, doing anything but this, Michael ran along the deck. The megalodon was done resisting, its carcass loose and soft, and its belly parted easily before the length of sharp metal.

A pink tsunami of guts and gore spilled forth across the deck, knocking the three men from their feet. Bits of half-digested and chewed up shark struck them like slaps to the face. Spluttering and cursing, Calvin struggled to rise just as a dark, heavy mass bowled him over. He wrestled with the thing, his limbs tangled around it. Michael saw the mass had a head, a man's head, rotten and mangled, attached to a torso which lacked arms or legs. Calvin wailed in terror, pushing the revenant away from him so that it flopped backwards, revealing the identity of the eaten man.

Michael recoiled in shock. It was Tom.

4

Gulf of Carpentaria, off the north coast of Australia, 2025

My guts clench like a fist. Taking a hold of my core, this fist shakes in angry denial, rattling my internal organs with physical trauma to match the roiling horror boiling in my psyche. Even as I stare at Tom's face—it's a torn up mask, mangled by shark teeth, rotten by sea water and stomach juices, the features barely recognisable—I can't believe it's him. I shake my head, mouth agape. It's like watching the resurrection of some zombie messiah, realising how horrifying that fable is when confronted with such a revenant in reality.

But Tom hasn't come to save us. He's a prophet of doom, a mirror in which we see our own deaths looming.

Michael, the corpse's dead eyes say to me in my thoughts, *this is what awaits you soon enough, devoured by everything you've sought after. You wanted freedom. This is freedom. Behold your reward for risking the hubris of the cruel sea.*

I don't know what to say back to those staring eyes, only that they're right. I have imagined my death, a story I invented, trying to manifest it into being. Every time I escaped into drugs was a small death, a way to relieve the burden of being alive, if only for a short time. And though the cuts were small, they added up to a grievous wound, one which has not yet healed for all the physical distance I have put between myself and my past. It's still present in my mind, true as ever, and looming close—a desire for the end to come, to be consumed by a way of life, to die living.

Drugs, fucking, fishing—myself, Sharna, Calvin—these are the holy trinity of ghosts sent to screw me over.

I envision them all as a black abyss, a huge mouth with jaws open wide, big enough for me to throw my whole life into, for me to walk through like a gate, with a promised release at the end which never comes. When I die something feeds on me, makes me into something new, flesh from flesh. Apex predators like the megalodon—like mankind—gather all life into the one life at the top of the pyramid. There they hang like a star in the firmament, a god in all but name, believing their existence is the reason for all the others below. Perhaps this is true, all the souls, flesh, and blood sucked up, used to create something huge, powerful, and beautiful.

I look at the corpse of the megalodon, just as mangled as Tom's, a deflated husk peppered with undignified wounds like a martyr. It seems holy now, a manifestation of the divine in its full glory, and we killed it. There's blood on my hands.

I wish it hadn't ended like this. Survivor's guilt wracks me, knowing Tom was a young man like me, though born in different circumstances. I don't deserve to live, not more than he does. I long for death now it has been denied to me. At least in nourishing the monster I could have been reborn as something new, vibrant, and truly alive in a way I can't seem to manifest for myself. I'm always trying to justify my existence through actions, chasing after outcomes which flee the more I run towards them. It's too exhausting. I want to curl up and die. I look at the spilt guts of the monster, the steam rising from the slit I have cut, and I take a step towards it. I will live on in the belly of the beast.

But the megalodon is dead, isn't it? I have cut my own throat, barred my own escape, no way back to the soft, warm folds of the womb. No mother to care for me, no flesh to embrace me. Even death is no way out anymore, all the little deaths I sought in drugs, or women, or even on this boat, are mirages.

***

"Fuck me and all," says Jords, leaning in close to inspect Tom's mangled corpse. "It's the boy. I told you something fucked up happened to him."

"My son!" wails Calvin, clutching at the body he was recoiling from a moment before, as if reunited after long years. But the corpse is nothing but a lifeless mannequin, a prop in a melodramatic play for Calvin's own benefit, his mind unable to bear the burden of his son's death, seeking to run from the responsibility of having brought a life into this world and failing to protect it.

"Stop that bullshit," I say as I get to my feet.

"Leave the captain to his grief," says Jords, crossing himself.

"If he cares so much about Tom, maybe he should have been kinder to him when he was still alive?"

"What the fuck would you know about it?" says Calvin around sobs. "What would you know about a father losing his son?"

I grimace, thinking of my dad. I can't imagine he cares if I live or die. If he did, he wouldn't have left.

"You killed him," I say to Calvin, my internal anger turning outwards.

"What the fuck did you say to me?" says Calvin, dropping Tom's corpse unceremoniously. He struggles to his feet, his bulk weighing heavy on him like an uneasy conscience. As he rises he clutches the shotgun—his talisman of power—shaking it like a shaman's voodoo stick over his son's corpse, as if this could bring him back. But Calvin doesn't have life in him, only death.

He turns on me. I back away, my skin tingling with rushing blood. My heartbeat pounds in my temples. In my hands is a red hot iron—the knife. I twist it so it catches the rays of the sun, flashing a sharp warning not to come closer.

"You don't think I'll gut you too? I've had quite a bit of practice lately," I say, nodding at the megalodon. I can't believe the words coming out of my mouth, the brazenness of them. But in Calvin I see my own dad, and I want revenge for the years of feeling unworthy of love. I can't run from it anymore, I have to stand and fight. Besides, there's nowhere to go on this boat, nowhere to hide. But if I can't get away neither can the ghost of my dad, here manifested in the form of this fat-headed bastard Calvin.

To the side Jords looks from me to the captain and back again, baring his rat teeth nervously. I wave the knife at him and he scampers away to hide behind the bulk of the megalodon. I laugh at his cowardice revealed, but the smile on my lips vanishes as I see what the captain is doing. With a meaty sausage finger he fishes the gunk out of the breaches of his shotgun, sliding in cartridges. He snaps the shotgun straight, raises the barrels. I stare into those two black holes and see the answer to all my problems. I lower the knife.

"You killed my son, not me," says Calvin. "You abandoned him."

"He told me to go to sleep," is all I can say, knowing it will do no good but wanting the truth to be the last thing said.

The final word goes to the megalodon, though, the cut slit in its guts burping like an obscene mouth. Out of this grotesque wound flows a wash of fresh bilgy junk which sloshes around our feet. In amongst it is a human arm, the skin mottled and blue. The hand of the thing is a clenched fist, its rigor mortis grip wrapped around a small object.

His curiosity getting the better of him, Calvin bends down to inspect the arm. It's obviously Tom's, but it's the object in the hand which has his attention. And mine too, my eyes locked on the closed fist. I start to tremble, the prospect of being killed with the shotgun nothing compared to the looming disaster I know is coming. I feel it like a weight bearing down on me, forcing me to bow to its might.

Calvin pokes at the hand with the tip of the shotgun.

"What the hell is that?" he says, frowning. He puts down the shotgun, takes a hold of his dead son's hand, attempting to open it. The dead fingers are unyielding claws. They do not bend, but snap like dry twigs sheathed in rotting flesh. The object tumbles free onto the deck, and I know what it is without even looking.

It's a corn cob pipe.

***

"Is that the fucking pipe the kid has being going on about for months?" asks Jords, jumping up and down to peek over the body of the megalodon like a naughty schoolboy spying over a fence. I don't have an answer for his question. It all seems so improbable, or even totally impossible, that this is my great-grandfather's pipe.

"My God," says Calvin, clutching the object and holding it up to the light as if inspecting a gold nugget he found in the ground. He rotates the thing between two fingers, and despite being dirty with gory muck, it does indeed shine amber yellow. He lowers it, his cold gaze turning to me. "You actually did it. You bloody killed him, didn't you?"

He throws the pipe at my feet, his face blossoming red with rage. My first response is to recoil from the object as if he'd tossed Tom's amputated arm instead— I'm just as horrified and disgusted. Even so, I bend over and scoop it up, like a puppet with its strings being pulled, and I can't help but wonder who the puppeteer is in such an automatic and reflexive action. The pipe is an insubstantial thing, light and small, but the implications of picking it up weigh heavily. To Calvin this is an admission of guilt. He puffs up like an indignant toad.

For reasons I cannot understand consciously, I put the disgusting pipe into my mouth. It tastes like salt water and putrid gut gasses, slimy on my lips. My teeth clink hard on it, the wood of the stem pliable yet resistant—it will give up no easy answers. Yet, like some voodoo psychometry—a psychic communion through touch—it speaks to me as I breathe in through it, tasting something oddly familiar and reassuring, despite the accompanying lingering disgust—disgust not only of it, but of myself and my past, made present through the nascent smell of tobacco and marijuana. There is a hot stink mixed in with it, the corpse breath of Tom, telling me how he died.

Even Calvin is thrown off-guard by my bizarre response, and he watches in puzzlement as I close my eyes. Even the tittering bird sounds of Jords, urging the captain to blow me away with the shotgun, fade into the blackness as day becomes night, and I see the world through Tom's eyes. I'm affected immediately by the statue-like sadness of the young man, cut through like the veins of marble with a determination to prove himself before an uncaring monolith, his father a sculpture which seems carved on such a grander scale, yet ultimately of the same shape—and this hurts even more, Tom knowing he can't escape the mould. In time he will become what he hates most.

I hear the siren's song of the sea, the burbling words which tell Tom of a release from all these troubles. There is an answer which promises a metamorphosis, a new life waiting on the other side of a dark veil. The sound is like a lure attached to a hook. It draws me—

sympathetically blended with Tom's experiences in the past—to leave the bridge, uncaring of the boat's controls, and go to the side of the ship. I can feel the strong breeze on my face, the hard railing against my stomach, and the cool water in my hand as I bend down to touch it.

A gift, the sea places the pipe into my hand, but then, in a cruel reversal, like the ebb and flow of the tides, the megalodon bursts from the water, a manifestation of the sea's will seeking compensation. With open jaws like a grasping hand, it grabs Tom in turn, exacting its price for its promise immediately. The jaws close like a gate snapping shut, exploding his head and killing him instantly. This is a merciful act, Tom never knowing anything but curiosity—piqued by the presence of the pipe—as he takes a step into the unknown.

***

I shudder, and it seems to me as if the shiver that reverberates through me also passes along the spine of the boat beneath my feet. My eyes snap open, lock onto the man opposite me. But Calvin is not looking at me, instead swivelling his fat head from side to side, the barrel of the shotgun aimed this way and that, as if he can't gauge in which direction the danger lies.

I don't hesitate, aware this man wants to kill me. Clenching my teeth, the pipe infects me with a rage not of my own. I take two steps forward. Calvin sees me coming, swings the shotgun up, but too slow. I thrust with the knife in my hand, stab it into his bulging gut. It slides in easily, sinking deep as if into pliant dough.

Jords makes a squeaking sound of surprise, unable to believe someone has been stabbed and that it was not him to do the stabbing—I share in this same sense of disjointed reality, having never expected this. Calvin himself only grunts in affirmation of the state of things, as if knowing it would come to this all along.

I let go of the blade's handle, stepping back as Calvin stumbles forward. His weight bears down on me like an avalanche of flesh folds. He shakes his fat head as if to deny death, one hand reaching for me, the other squeezing the trigger of the shotgun. But the barrel has drifted lazily downwards, Calvin's strength sapped by pain, and it goes off into the deck. The shot is louder than I expect, and makes the whole boat rock. Jords squeaks again and runs back and forth in a panic, but he's not getting anywhere.

There's nowhere for me to run either. Calvin grabs me around the collar of my shirt, forces me up against the megalodon carcass. "You fucking piece of shit," he spits in my face.

I buck my body, trying to squirm out from under him. I feel something hard give way against my thrashing, and, like I struck a lever which deactivates an automaton, Calvin goes stiff, his eyes blank with overloaded signals from his body. He makes a rasping sound, dice shaken in the cup of his mouth. The death rattle shudders through his whole body, shaking his belly blubber like jelly. His fat head folds backwards, and, chin pointed skywards, he keels over backwards. As he hits the deck with a thudding squelch I see the knife has completely disappeared inside him—a dark hole in his cannonball stomach oozes blood and foul juices. In my struggles I'd pushed the weapon in handle and all, the length of steel having found the kidneys for a paralysing, fatal blow.

I wipe sweat off my brow. My breath saws in and out of my lungs in rough gusts like a rusty set of bellows. I feel dizzy, my vision pulsing as my heart beats hard like a countdown to my doom. I grab at my chest in an attempt to arrest its pounding, trying to tell it the danger has passed. But it doesn't believe me, some sixth sense keeping my body heightened. I look around for the source of the danger and see a head peering over the megalodon. Jords bares his rat teeth with a snarl.

"You killed the bloody captain, you mongrel," he says excitedly, his head bobbing up and down like a buoy in the water. "You wait until I get my hands on you."

He clambers awkwardly up the far side of the monster, scattering the birds which have gathered to peck at the carcass as it rots in the stinking heat of the sun. Gaining the summit, there he balances awkwardly on the slimy surface, looking uncertain on how to proceed.

"I wish I had my knife. Then I'd do for you," he says, biting his lips nervously, looking around for an answer. His darting, ping pong eyes settle on the shotgun in Calvin's dead hand. A murderous smile splits his face like a dirty pink wound.

My adrenaline spikes. I turn to move, everything happening in slow motion as if I'm running underwater. I'm struck around the ears by another booming bang. This time I know it's not from the shotgun. The deck lurches under my feet, a bucking amusement park ride which sends the shotgun skittering away from me. I chase after it clumsily, having to jump over the great mound of Calvin's corpse to do so. Jords sees me doing this, and it goads him to action. He takes a single step forward, losing his footing as he does, and slides down the grey, slimy side of the monster. The corpse of the captain breaks his fall. Calvin lets out a long, sad wheeze like a broken bagpipe.

"Sorry, Captain," says Jords, floundering like a dropped fish as he tries to get up. I turn back to give him a kick in the chest just as he's finding his feet. He is sent sprawling, face-planting on the deck. When he flips onto his back, his face is a bloody mask, nose flattened to one side. "Oi, cunt, I'll fucking kill you for that," he says, his voice even more nasal than before.

I ignore him, go after the shotgun again. But as I'm about to grab it, the whole boat heaves under me, tilting at a steep angle, the stern up in the air. I'm sent sliding along the length of the deck, colliding with Jords as he scrambles up towards me, sending us both into a tangled heap against the outside wall of the cabin.

"What the hell is going on?" says Jords. We both have our hands on the shotgun, trying to wrestle it free of each other's grip as the boat settles once more with a huge salty splash.

"It's another megalodon, you idiot!" I scream through clenched teeth. I'm still biting hard on the corn cob pipe and only process the words myself as they escape my lips. I don't know who put those words into my mouth, but I know they're true. As if in affirmation, the boat is violently shunted ten metres sideways. I hear timbers snapping and steel screeching as it tears.

Jords and I look at each other. The awareness dawns in both our eyes that there's no need to kill each other.

We're already dead.

***

This doesn't stop Jords fighting for the shotgun, and he pulls it from my hands with desperate strength. Rather than turn it on me, though, he rushes to the side of the boat, points the weapon down at the water.

"Oh, fuck!" he shrieks, firing the gun. The blast is lost in a roar of water as the megalodon bursts from the sea. It's a colossal monster, all teeth and massive bulk. The gargantuan dorsal fin eclipses the sun. Gaping jaws hinge open impossibly wide. The long, heavy body arches up to loom over the boat despite its tail still being in the water.

To live in its dark shadow is to die.

Jords screams in mortal terror—the shot from the shotgun merely ricochets off the megalodon's toughened, grey hide, not even slowing it as it bears down on him like a runaway truck. Scornful of mankind's weapons, the prehistoric shark unleashes its own evolutionary wonders, row after row of razor sharp teeth as long as swords. Jords' scream is cut off with a percussive slap of bone on bone as the jaws snap closed on him like the cruelly-spiked doors of an iron maiden. The megalodon doesn't just bite into his body, it pulverises Jords with explosive force. The massive impaling spikes of teeth slice clean through with no resistance. They rupture flesh into goblets of gore, squash bone into powder. A red mist is thrown up in the air like spray from the sea as Jords bursts like a balloon.

The megalodon lands on the deck with brutal force, flattening the already deflated corpse of its kin. The whole boat plunges down into the water under the weight and I lose my footing. Scrambling onto my hands and knees, I look up, straight into the eye of the monster. It's a moist black marble rolling around, cold, dark, menacing. My guts turn to ice as it fixates on me with a jerk of movement. To look into this pitiless orb is to witness an ancient intelligence, alien to my own, seeing me as nothing but meat. They are the eyes of a merciless killer.

And yet, as it writhes around, skin on skin with the dead megalodon, I get a sense of something more complicated, something I never would have expected from such a monster. The massive size of this megalodon compared to the one we killed tells a story. A mother comes to save its child in distress. Arriving too late, it grieves...

…and seeks bloody vengeance.

***

With explosive energy, the megalodon flexes like a bent spring and then straightens, throwing its huge body weight up the deck towards me. There is no time to run, nowhere to go. I try to scream, but my lungs are empty, the air knocked out of them as the nose of the monster rams into my chest, a battering ram which snaps ribs like twigs. I'm thrown by the blow, smashing into the cabin wall. I feel more bones break, but adrenaline surges through me, and I get to my feet in time to see my looming death.

The chomping jaws of the megalodon churn the air like a giant industrial mincing machine. The teeth are stained with blood. I can smell the corpse stink wafting up from the pink gullet. There is a black hole at its centre—a lifeless abyss where I must surely soon go, never to return.

I turn and open the cabin door. Stairs lead down into another dark space, but I have no other options. I stumble and trip as I descend them. I hear a clicking sound following me down. Turning, I see the corn cob pipe haunts me still, tumbling down the steps in a surge of sea water.

I scoop down to pick it up as the whole cabin rocks—the trawler caught in a stormy tempest as the megalodon bounces its weight up and down, squirming like a worm along the deck. I go deeper into the bowels of the boat, down towards an illusionary safety.

There is no longer any escape.

***

The top part of the cabin is ripped off as if by the winds of a cyclone. The megalodon rends and tears in its grief-stricken fury. Wood splinters under the impact of its bucking body and teeth shred steel as if it were nothing but aluminium foil.

Eyes darting in panic, I seek a way out of an impossible situation, instincts driving me to try to survive even as all seems hopeless. I stick the pipe in my mouth unconsciously, but this makes things worse. How I wish for one last smoke. If only I had a bit of weed to relax me, ease my screaming nerves, I could at least face the end at peace. Instead, I'm a jangling mess, overwhelmed by terror.

In my panic I fling open a closet and hurl myself inside. Closing the door behind me blocks all light, sealing my own coffin.

***

Shallow, painful breaths, eyes blinking in the dark, teeth locked tight on the thin stem of the pipe, skin raw and burning with adrenaline, mind scattered and unable to think, broken ribs like knives in the chest—these are some of my last sensations as water floods through the cracks of the door and begins to fill up the closet.

***

The boat is sinking. I spit out the corn cob pipe, rejecting it once and for all as I tilt back my head to suck in one last breath of life before the rising water engulfs my head. I am entombed in cold, dark wetness. Seconds feel like hours, stretching forever. The screaming pain in my lungs is replaced by a tingling euphoria which spreads over my entire body, and I finally find some of that peace I sought for so long. Numbness overcomes me, bright stars bursting like celebratory fireworks in the black void of my existence as my brain is starved of oxygen.

The irony of drowning instead of being eaten by the megalodon escapes me as I lose all sensation.

I feel nothing as huge jaws clamp down to smash the closet open and rip me in half.

Check out other great

Sea Monster Novels!

Michael Cole

SCAR

Scar is a killing machine. Born from DNA spliced between the extinct Megalodon and modern day Great White, he has a viciousness that transcends time. His evil is reflected in his eyes, his savagery in his two-inch serrated teeth, his ruthlessness in his trail of death. After escaping captivity, the killer shark travels to the island community Cross Point, where prey is in abundance. With an insatiable appetite, heightened senses, and skin impervious to bullets, Scar kills everything that crosses his path. His reign of terror puts him at war with the island sheriff, Nick Piatt. With the body count rising, Nick vows to protect his island community from the vicious threat. With the aid of a marine biologist, a rookie deputy, and a bad-tempered fisherman, Nick leads a crusade against Scar, as well as the ruthless scientist who created him.

Rick Chesler

HOTEL MEGALODON

An underwater luxury hotel on a gorgeous tropical island is set for an extravagant opening weekend with the world watching. The only thing standing in the way of a first-rate experience for the jet-setting VIPs is an unscrupulous businessman and sixty feet of prehistoric shark. As the underwater complex is besieged by a marauding behemoth, newly minted marine biologist Coco Keahi must face off against the ancient predator as it rises from the deep with a vengeance. Meanwhile, a human monster has decided he would be better off if Coco were one of the creature's victims.

Check out other great
Sea Monster Novels!

Michael Cole
CREATURE OF LAKE SHADOW

It was supposed to be a simple bank robbery. Quick. Clean. Efficient. It was none of those. With police searching for them across the state, a band of criminals hide out in a desolate cabin on the frozen shore of Lake Shadow. Isolated, shrouded in thick forest, and haunted by a mysterious history, they thought it was the perfect place to hide. Tensions mount as they hear strange noises outside. Slain animals are found in the snow. Before long, they realize something is watching them. Something hungry, violent, and not of this world. In their attempt to escape, they found the Creature of Lake Shadow.

C.J. Waller
PREDATOR X

When deep level oil fracking uncovers a vast subterranean sea, a crack team of cavers and scientists are sent down to investigate. Upon their arrival, they disappear without a trace. A second team, including sedimentologist Dr Megan Stoker, are ordered to seek out Alpha Team and report back their findings. But Alpha team are nowhere to be found – instead, they are faced with something unexpected in the depths. Something ancient. Something huge. Something dangerous. Predator X

Check out other great

Sea Monster Novels!

Matt James

SUB-ZERO

The only thing colder than the Antarctic air is the icy chill of death... Off the coast of McMurdo Station, in the frigid waters of the Southern Ocean, a new species of Antarctic octopus is unintentionally discovered. Specialists aboard a state-of-the-art DARPA research vessel aim to apply the animal's "sub-zero venom" to one of their projects: An experimental painkiller designed for soldiers on the front lines. All is going according to plan until the ship is caught in an intense storm. The retrofitted tanker is rocked, and the onboard laboratory is destroyed. Amid the chaos, the lead scientist is infected by a strange virus while conducting the specimen's dissection. The scientist didn't die in the accident. He changed.

Alister Hodge

THE CAVERN

When a sink hole opens up near the Australian outback town of Pintalba, it uncovers a pristine cave system. Sam joins an expedition to explore the subterranean passages as paramedic support, hoping to remain unneeded at base camp. But, when one of the cavers is injured, he must overcome paralysing claustrophobia to dive pitch-black waters and squeeze through the bowels of the earth. Soon he will find there are fates worse than being buried alive, for in the abandoned mines and caves beneath Pintalba, there are ravenous teeth in the dark. As a savage predator targets the group with hideous ferocity, Sam and his friends must fight for their lives if they are ever to see the sun again.